MILF & *Cookies*

MILF & Cookies

A Small-Town Romance Scandal to DIE
For

Ray Gray

ISBN: 979-8-9949939-0-3
First Edition

Cover design by Ray Gray
Interior formatting by Ray Gray

Printed in the United States of America

Published by THE COLLYNS GROUP LLC

For anyone who has ever been too much and decided to stay that way. For my daughter, who I do it all for. And, for the badass women who rebuild themselves anyway.

This novel contains themes of divorce, harassment, and threats involving a child.

Reader discretion advised.

Chapter One
Return of the Hot Mess

There's no manual for moving back to your hometown after a divorce.

No checklist. No TED Talk. No "Divorce for Dummies" that explains what to do when you find yourself crying in a U-Haul while eating gas station donuts and your seven-year-old asks if the dog gets joint custody too.

It had been years at this point.

I tried to make living in the city work for us…

I couldn't. It's hard managing when you're alone. And for 7 years, I was alone.

There's just me.

And Piper.

And a glittery notebook labeled Operation MILF & Cookies sitting boldly on the dashboard like a dare. Which, in retrospect, probably wasn't the best branding decision while parked outside a Baptist church. But subtlety has never been my thing. Subtlety is how you end up ten years into a marriage where you've slowly erased yourself in polite increments.

I pull into Willow Creek's town square and immediately feel it — the weight of memory pressing against the windshield.

The courthouse clock. The diner with the chipped blue awning. The park where I once swore I'd never come

back after graduation because I was destined for something bigger.

And here I am.

Bigger? Debatable.

Divorced? Absolutely.

"Mom?" Piper's voice floats from the backseat. "Why are your eyes leaking?"

I blink hard and wipe my cheek with the heel of my hand. "They're not leaking. They're… preheating."

She narrows her eyes in the rearview mirror. She inherited that look from me. The one that says I know you're lying but I'll let you have dignity.

"Do you want some Gushers?" she asks.

I nod.

She hands me three like a rationed emotional support system.
This is how we roll now.

Small town.

Small apartment.
Small budget.
Big feelings.

As we drive past the elementary school, something tugs at my brain.

A flicker.

A weird, hollow déjà vu that makes my chest tighten.

The school looks… smaller than I remember. Or maybe I'm just bigger.

So I just shake it off. Trauma does weird things to your sense of scale.

I'd become a recluse. I stopped visiting family. I stopped answering friends. It took me seven whole years to figure out how to be alone again.

Well. Alone-ish.

There was Piper, of course.

But motherhood isn't the same as partnership. And somewhere along the way, I forgot how to be a woman outside of survival mode.

The bakery space is worse than the photos.

Peeling paint curls at the corners like it's trying to escape. The front window has a crack shaped vaguely like Florida. The back room smells like expired cinnamon and something older. Something tired.

But it has bones.
High ceilings.
Brick walls.
Natural light.
Possibility.

And right now, it's mine.

I step inside slowly, heels echoing against dusty tile. This is sacred ground.

Or it will be.

The kind of sacred ground where dreams either live loudly or die quietly depending on how fast you learn commercial plumbing.

"Is this the oven?" Piper asks, pointing at a rusted beast in the corner.

I nod. "It is."

She studies it seriously. "Is it haunted?"

"Emotionally? Probably."

She hums thoughtfully and pulls out her sketchpad.

"Okay. We'll need glitter. And a frosting gun. And maybe a piñata shaped like a butt." I just laugh before I can stop myself. This is the part where most single moms would panic.

The *debt*.
The *risk*.
The *rent*.
The *whispers*.

But I'm not most moms.

I'm a woman who spent ten years folding herself smaller and softer and quieter so a man wouldn't feel threatened by her ambition. I'm a woman who was told — gently, politely, repeatedly — that confidence looked better in "moderation." I'm done moderating. Even if it kills me. Even if I fail publicly. Even if Willow Creek watches the whole thing like a spectator sport.

I walk to the front window and press my palm against the glass. Across the street, the courthouse steps glow in late afternoon light. And for just a second — I have the strangest sensation that someone is watching me.

I glance over my shoulder.

Nothing.

Just dust motes and ambition. So I shake it off. Moving does that. Makes you paranoid.

Later that week, I'm waist-deep in tile samples and paint swatches when the sign guy shows up.

"Just confirming," he says casually, "the name you want on the front is… MILF & Cookies?"

I pause and I glance at Piper.

She shrugs. "You already told everyone on Facebook."

Right.

I exhale. "Yep. That's the one."

He doesn't blink. Just writes it down. Gen Z contractors. Immune to scandal.

After he leaves, Piper tilts her head at me.

"Mom," she says carefully. "What does MILF mean?"

I freeze.

"It means…" I scramble. "Mom I'd Like to… Feed."

She squints.

"That sounds fake."

"It's aspirational branding."

She accepts this. Kids are so generous with trust. And, I hope I deserve it.

The soft opening is in five days. The espresso machine hisses at me like it knows I'm bluffing.
The flour delivery is late. The fridge makes a noise that sounds suspiciously like a dying whale.

And last night, I accidentally baked a batch of "Oops All Butter" cookies that melted into a single terrifying mega-biscuit that looked like regret.

But Piper believes in me.

She made a flyer. It's in crayon but who's judging?

It says:

MY MOM IS A BAKER AND SHE'S HOT.

I consider correcting it BUT I don't. The next day she tapes it to the post office bulletin board. By dinner, three people have messaged asking what kind of "establishment" I'm opening.

Small towns move fast.

I stand in the middle of my half-painted bakery that night, exhausted and smelling like sugar and hope, and whisper into the empty room:

"You better work."

And for just a second —

The flicker of neon reflection in the cracked glass looks like a pulse. Like something alive. Like something waiting.

I ignore the chill down my spine.

I have bigger things to fear than ghosts.

Chapter Two
Freshly Single, Lightly Unhinged

If a box of wine, a Pinterest vision board, and a midlife crisis had a baby —

It would be MILF & Cookies.

And honestly? That tracks.

I'm standing on a ladder adjusting the hot pink neon sign when it flickers.

MILF.

It hums softly, like it's judging me.

Same, girl.

I climb down slowly, legs shaking from more than exertion. Three weeks ago, I was living in a condo I didn't decorate, married to a man who barely looked up from his phone at dinner. Now I'm divorced, broke, and supergluing shelving units at midnight while googling "how long does regret last?"

Forward motion.
That's what we're calling it.

"Mommy?"

Piper emerges from the back hallway holding a glitter soap dispenser.

"There's confetti in the toilet."

"Whimsical ambiance," I reply automatically.

She nods like that's logical and I kneel to wipe frosting from her cheek. She doesn't know how scared I am. She doesn't know that I wake up at 3 a.m. every night with my heart racing and the overwhelming fear that I've made a mistake so large it will swallow us whole. She doesn't know that sometimes when I close my eyes, I smell antiseptic.

Hospital clean.

Metallic.

Like something important happened there and I just…
can't reach it.

I shake the thought away because divorce does weird
things to your brain. You lose chunks of yourself.
Memories blur.

It's normal.

— Probably.

The name makes people laugh. Or blush. Or send passive-
aggressive emails.

But I like it.

MILF & Cookies is about reclaiming the parts of myself I
was told to tuck away.

The softness.
The sexiness.
The hunger.
The ambition.

I spent years trying to be digestible. Now I want to be
unforgettable.

"Mommy," Piper says, staring at a tray of cinnamon
shortbread shaped like peach emojis.

"The cookies look nervous."

"They should be," I mutter. "Today's the day they meet
capitalism."

The bell above the door jingles.

And then he walks in.

Pressed khakis. Structured jaw. Button-down shirt that has
never known a chaotic laundry day.

He scans the space like it's a hazard assessment.

I instantly dislike him.

And also notice everything about him.

"Hi there," I say. "Can I help you?"

"You're the owner?"

"Unfortunately, yes."

"I'm Graham Walsh. PTA President."

My stomach drops.

Oh no.

He gestures to the sign. "This is… bold."

"Thank you."

"It's suggestive."
"It's empowering."

"It's a lawsuit."

"It's branding."

He doesn't smile.

I grab a brownie anyway and offer it to him on a napkin
that says Eat Me.

He does not eat it.
I watch him watching the space.

The counters.

The labels.
The kitchen door.

Assessing.

For a brief second, something strange flickers through me.
A memory of being evaluated.

Not by him.

By someone else. A woman with calm eyes and steady hands.

I blink.
It's gone.

"Is this how you want to represent yourself?" he asks quietly. "To the school?"

It lands harder than I want it to.

The old voice rises.

Too *much*. Too *loud*. Too

unstable.

But I bury it.

I lean forward.

"Yeah," I say. "It is."

He looks at me for a beat too long.

And for a second —

I don't see judgment. I see curiosity. And maybe something else.

When he leaves, I stand very still.

Piper hands me a cookie that says BOY BYE in sprinkles and I take a bite.

It's slightly burnt.

But so am I.

Chapter Three
PTA
Ain't Ready

The sign still haunted him.

He could see it even now, burned behind his eyelids like a neon afterimage.

MILF & Cookies.

In hot pink.
In cursive.
Humming with flickering light and poor decision-making.

Graham sipped his black coffee and stared down the long, glossy conference table in the Willow Creek Elementary staff lounge, which had been hastily converted into a "community planning hub" — PTA code for folding chairs, stale cookies, and passive-aggressive moms in coordinated athleisure.

Across from him, Mindy Clayborn was reviewing the Bake-Off budget like she was presenting at a shareholder meeting.

He half-listened. Half-tried not to imagine frosting on collarbones.

Jesus Christ.

He rubbed the back of his neck and reminded himself why he cared.

Structure.
Order.
Stability.

Things his son, Miles, needed.

Things he needed.

Not cupcakes shaped like peach emojis and a woman who thought sarcasm counted as customer service.

"I just think," Mindy was saying now, voice tight with controlled disapproval, "that if we're allowing vendors like her to participate in the Bake-Off this year, we should revisit event branding. It's a family event. Not a… bachelor party."

A few moms nodded.

Graham kept his expression neutral, even as his jaw tightened.

He'd known the bakery would become a problem the second he saw it. Knew Sloane Matthews would stir things up the way only a woman in glitter Crocs and red lipstick could.

But now that she was in PTA orbit?

She was disruption. And disruption had consequences. He didn't have the emotional bandwidth for consequences.

Not after the hospital.

Not after loss.

Not after learning firsthand that wanting something badly enough was the fastest way to lose it.

He cleared his throat.

"We can't remove her from the Bake-Off because she's unconventional," he said evenly. "She's compliant with vendor regulations."

Mindy arched a brow. "You sound defensive."

He wasn't. He was objective. There was a difference. Before he could redirect the conversation to allergy labeling requirements, the lounge door opened.
And there she was.

Late.

Bright.
Carrying sugar like it was a personality trait.

Sloane Matthews stepped inside with a bakery box in one hand and coffee in the other, oversized cardigan slipping off one shoulder like she didn't care who noticed.

She definitely cared. That was what surprised him.

"Sorry I'm late," she said cheerfully. "Had to frost a few things and emotionally recover from glitter trauma. Carry on."

A couple moms snorted, but Mindy did not. Graham forced himself not to stare at the powdered sugar smudged along Sloane's cheekbone.

She was performing.

He saw it now.

The jokes were armor.
The flirtation was deflection.
The exaggerated confidence was a shield.

He recognized that energy.

It was the same one he'd worn after the hospital. After the kind of night that fractures your life clean down the middle. He hated that he recognized it.

"We were discussing logistics," he said stiffly.

"Love that for us," she replied, sliding into the empty chair across from him. "Also I brought buttered bourbon blondies. Gluten-free-ish. Emotionally therapeutic."

She opened the box. The scent alone should have required a permit.

"Ms. Matthews," Mindy began sharply, "we're addressing concerns about appropriateness."

Sloane widened her eyes. "Do you want a cookie or a hug? I offer both."

More laughter.

Graham risked another glance at her.

Her smile was too wide.

Her shoulders too tight.

She was bracing.

Interesting.

"I also heard we need a Bake-Off co-chair," she continued lightly. "I volunteer as tribute."

Principal Navarro looked down at his clipboard.

"You're already listed," he said. "Co-chairing with Graham."

The room went silent. Sloane blinked. "Excuse me?"

Graham straightened. "That must be an error."

"Nope," Navarro said cheerfully. "You'll coordinate vendors and sponsorships. First meeting Friday."

Their eyes met across the table.

There it was again. That jolt. Not lust. Not exactly.

Recognition.

"I hope you like frosting," she said.

"I don't eat sugar."

Her smile turned wicked. "Even worse. You're uptight and joyless."

"And you're reckless with a fondant addiction."

Her eyebrow lifted. "That was oddly specific."

He looked away first. He wasn't losing composure over a bakery owner with questionable branding. He refused.

Later, in the art room, sunlight poured through tall windows and painted everything gold.

Sloane sat backward in a chair, flipping through his laminated spreadsheet like it was a foreign artifact.

"Is this color-coded?" she asked.

"Yes."

"Did you laminate it?"

"I find it helpful."

She blinked slowly. "I feel like I should've brought a protractor."

He ignored her.

She kept reading. Then she paused.

"Okay," she said quietly. "This is good. Allergy symbols. Booth spacing. Time slots."

He hesitated. "Thank you."

"I mean, it's overkill," she added with a grin. "But sexy overkill."

"Please don't refer to my spreadsheets as sexy."

"Too late."

He hated that she amused him. Hated it more that he wanted to see what she'd say next.

"I was thinking," she continued, more serious now, "we could add a kids' tasting table. Sugar-free samples. Maybe a bake-your-own station."

He studied her. No sarcasm. No wink. Just… effort.

"I know I'm not exactly PTA Barbie," she added, softer. "But I do want this to go well."

There it was. The crack in the armor. Not chaos. Not recklessness.

He cleared his throat. "That's a good idea."

Her eyes widened slightly. "Are you agreeing with me?"

"Don't make it weird."

"Too late."

The art room door creaked open. Piper burst in first, tiara crooked. Miles followed behind, clutching a half-finished sketch.

"We found you!" Piper announced.

Sloane was already unrolling paper, handing out smocks, making space.

"You good with paint, Miles?" she asked.
Miles nodded. "I like drawing spaceships."

"Then this is your moment, kid."

Graham watched carefully.

Watched how she knelt to Miles' level.
Watched how she didn't talk down to him.
Watched how Piper glowed under her attention.

"She thinks your mom is magic," Miles said quietly.

Graham looked at his son. Then at Sloane, who was currently biting open a paint tube with her teeth. "She might be," he said before he could stop himself. Across the room, she looked up and caught him watching.

Her expression shifted "soft"

"You okay, Walsh?" she asked.

He wasn't. He was aware — suddenly, dangerously aware — that she wasn't chaos.She was gravity.

And gravity pulls.

And pulling leads to wanting. And wanting leads to losing.

He had learned that lesson already. He wasn't volunteering to relearn it. Across the hallway window, late sunlight reflected off glass. For a split second, Graham thought he saw someone standing near the parking lot.

Still.

Watching.

He blinked.

The figure was gone.

Probably nothing.

Just light.

Just nerves.

He told himself that.

But later that night, when he drove past her bakery on the way home, he slowed down without meaning to.

The neon flickered once.

Like a pulse.

Like something alive.

And for reasons he couldn't explain, the back of his neck prickled. He kept driving. But he didn't stop thinking about her. And that worried him more than the sign ever could.

Graham did not believe in chaos.

He believed in schedules. In laminated charts. In bedtime at exactly 8:15 p.m. In apples sliced evenly because symmetry mattered.

Chaos was what happened the night Miles was born.

The hospital hallway smelled like antiseptic and burnt coffee. His ex-wife screamed at him for breathing too loud. A nurse told him to sit down. He didn't.

He stood.

Because if he sat, he might unravel.

He had thought fatherhood would feel like control. Like stepping into something solid. Instead it felt like watching a storm build and realizing he didn't know how to hold the roof down.

When Miles finally cried, small and furious and alive, something inside Graham cracked open.

Not loudly.

Not dramatically.

Just enough to let fear in.

Fear that he wouldn't be enough.

Fear that if he loosened his grip even slightly, something would slip through his fingers and disappear.

That night, holding his son for the first time, Graham made himself a promise:

No chaos.
No instability.
No mess.

Structure was love.
Predictability was protection.

And then Sloane Matthews opened a bakery called MILF & Cookies and laughed in the face of every rule he built his life around.

And God help him, it didn't feel like destruction.

It felt like oxygen.

Chapter 4
Batter Up

You know what no one tells you about "starting over"? It still feels like failure. Even when you slap a glittery label on it and drizzle bourbon frosting over the top. Even when you post filtered photos and caption them with things like fresh start! and watch me rise!

Failure has a flavor.

Metallic.
Warm.
Humiliating.

It lingers in the back of your throat no matter how much sugar you dump on top of it.

And I hate that.
Because I'm not supposed to be ashamed.

I'm supposed to be empowered.

The woman who left the cheating husband.
The woman who opened her own business.
The woman who shows up to PTA meetings in combat boots and lipstick and makes suburban moms clutch their pearls.

But sometimes? Sometimes I just feel tired. And judged. And sticky. (Because Piper dumped an entire bottle of maple syrup behind the fridge and I still haven't found it.)

So when Graham Walsh looks at me like I'm chaos in human form, I tell myself it doesn't matter.

His approval isn't currency I need.

He's just a grumpy man in Patagonia fleece with trauma and a clipboard.

And then he texts me.

At 9:47 p.m.

About *muffins*.

And I spiral.
"I'm just saying," I whisper to myself as I lie sideways across my bed in a frosting-stained tee, "if you're going to pick a fight, at least buy something first."

My phone buzzes again.

GRAHAM: What the hell is a "Hot Mess Scone"?

I grin despite myself.

SLOANE: It's a pastry with broken dreams and red pepper flakes.

GRAHAM: Why red pepper flakes?

SLOANE: Because pain is part of the healing process.

There's a pause.

Then:

GRAHAM: …that actually makes sense.

I blink.

Did Graham Walsh just validate my metaphor? This man once corrected my grammar in a parent group chat. I sit

up in bed. My pulse does something stupid. Because validation from the wrong man still hits like dopamine, apparently. I hate that about myself.

Earlier That Day

The art room smells like tempera paint and impending bad decisions.

Piper and Miles are in the corner building what they've decided is a "Robot Defense System," which appears to be cardboard with strategically placed googly nipple shields.

"I think we broke them," I murmur, nodding toward the robot.
Graham glances over and laughs.

Not a polite huff.

Not a forced PTA chuckle.

An *actual* laugh.

It hits me in the stomach.

"I'll alert the authorities," he says.

I stare at him. "Was that sarcasm?"

"Careful," he replies. "I'm not a beginner like you."

I squint. "You're a very confusing man."

He studies me for a moment longer than necessary and then explains, "You're a very loud woman."
I grin. "Thank you."

"It wasn't a compliment."

"Yes, it was. You just don't know how to admit it."

He doesn't argue. But, he doesn't look away either. And that's when the tension shifts. Because when he looks at me like that — not irritated, not judging, just curious — I feel exposed. Seen. Like maybe he's clocked the fact that I'm performing half the time. That I crack jokes because silence is dangerous. Because in silence, I think. And when I think, I remember.

The hospital waiting room.
The smell of antiseptic.
A woman sitting beside me saying something calm and reassuring.

I blink.

The memory dissolves before I can grab it. Stress does that.
I clear my throat. "We should probably finish sorting vendor tables before I start naming booths after sexual regrets."

His lip twitches.

I catch it.

Score one for the hot mess.
After closing.
After scrubbing icing off the mixer.
After telling Piper the dramatic bedtime saga of The Great Brownie Fiasco of Kindergarten.

I stare at the ceiling.

And feel… Off.

Like something is humming just beneath my skin. I send the text before I can stop myself.

SLOANE: Real question. Does my bakery make me look unprofessional?
I instantly regret it.

Too vulnerable.

Too honest.

The bubbles appear.

Disappear.

Reappear.

My stomach knots.

GRAHAM: No. It makes you look alive.

Alive.

That word lands somewhere tender.

SLOANE: That sounds like a compliment.

GRAHAM: It is.

My throat tightens.

I type slower this time.

SLOANE: You ever feel like the version of you everyone sees isn't actually you?

Long pause.
Longer than before.

I almost throw my phone across the room. Then

—

GRAHAM: Every day.

Something cracks open inside me.

SLOANE: Sometimes I feel like I'm always performing.
If I stop being funny or loud or sexy or interesting, I'll
just disappear.

The typing bubble sits there.

Then vanishes.

Then returns.

GRAHAM: Sometimes I wish I could disappear. You
remind me what it looks like not to.

I close my eyes.

Because that's too much.

Too real.

I hold my phone to my chest like I'm sixteen and terrified
of breaking a spell.

Something is happening.

Something dangerous.

I unlock the bakery before sunrise. The air inside is cool
and quiet. And on the counter—
A coffee.
Oat milk latte.
My name written neatly on the side.

A sticky note:

You don't have to perform for me.
— G

I stare at it for a long time. No one has ever said that to me before. And that scares me more than judgment ever could.

Outside, through the cracked front window, I catch movement across the street.

A car idling.

I squint.

The car pulls away.

Probably nothing.

Just early morning traffic.

I take a sip of the coffee and tell myself I'm not already in too deep.

Chapter Five
Sweet Like Sin

There are exactly four things I know to be true:

1. Baking is therapy.
2. Cupcakes are a love language.
3. If you use salted butter for pie crust, you're probably emotionally repressed.
4. And Graham Walsh is the hottest person I've ever fantasized about hitting with a rolling pin.
Which is unfortunate.

Because he's in my kitchen.

Sleeves rolled.

Apron on.
Forearms out.

Looking like a guilt-ridden lumberjack who wandered into a Nancy Meyers movie and forgot how to smile.

And worse?

He brought **ingredients**.

"I pre-measured the sugar," he says, placing a labeled bag on the counter. "And sifted the flour."

I blink.

"You sifted."

"Yes."

"Voluntarily?"

"I like precision."

Jesus Christ.

I stare at the supplies.

He alphabetized the vanilla extracts.
"You reorganized my spice rack."

"They were inconsistent."

"Graham, are you being held hostage by Martha Stewart?"

He pinches the bridge of his nose. "Do you narrate your thoughts out loud?"

"Only when repressing sexual tension."

His head jerks up.

I grin.

He mutters something about boundaries. But he doesn't leave.

That's the problem.

Piper and Miles are decorating cupcakes at the side table.

Piper has added one thousand edible eyeballs to a frosting swirl and named it "Lady Cupcake Murderface."

Miles is building a fondant shield like he's preparing for battle.

Piper immediately decided Miles was "too serious for his own good," which in Piper language meant she'd adopted him.

Miles, on the other hand, studied her like she was a science experiment with glitter.

"You're not supposed to run in the hallway," he told her. She ran backward. He sighed and followed.

That was the beginning.

By recess, they were arguing about whether dragons were real and by lunch, they'd decided to build a cupcake business empire "but without alcohol because we are minors."

Miles made spreadsheets. Piper designed logos with swords. I watched it happen like something fragile forming in real time. Two kids who didn't quite fit anywhere suddenly fitting with each other.

Graham watches them. His shoulders soften.

"You ever bake with Miles?" I ask gently.

He hesitates.

"His mom used to."

The air changes.

I nod. I don't push. But, I notice the way he grips the counter a little tighter.
There's grief there.

Deep.

Old.

Still sharp.

I recognize it. Because mine smells like antiseptic and unanswered questions. And sometimes, late at night, I swear I can hear a voice telling me everything will be okay. But I don't remember who said it.

I shake it off.

Focus.

"Okay," I say brightly. "Final bake-off contenders."

Tequila Lime Tragedy Tartlets.
The One Night Stand Shortbread.
Raspberry Regret Bars.

"Do all your desserts come with trauma flashbacks?" he asks.
"Only the good ones."

He tastes one.

Closes his eyes.

"That's… incredible."

I bow. "Coping mechanism."

He studies me.

"You use humor to deflect."

"Wow. That's both accurate and extremely rude."

"What are you scared of?" he asks quietly.

The question lands hard.

I want to joke.

I don't.

"Failing," I admit. "Being seen trying and still not being good enough."

He nods slowly.

"Same."

The honesty is electric.

We're too close.

Flour dusting the air.

Breath warm.

His fingers brush mine reaching for the piping bag.

I freeze.

He doesn't.
He looks at me like I'm something breakable.

Or dangerous.

Or both.

And just as his hand slides to my jaw—

"MOM! MILES GLUED AN EYEBALL TO THE DOG'S BUTT!"

We jump apart. Sugarloaf trots past with a frosting eyeball attached to her tail. Romantic tension: ruined.

But not erased.

That night, I dream again but it's not in full images. Just flashes.

A hospital corridor.
A man in a suit standing near a vending machine.
A woman in scrubs smiling at me.

I wake up with my heart racing.

I don't know why.

chapter six
Cracks
in the
glaze

Graham had always believed that if he could control the variables, he could control the outcome.

Spreadsheets. Schedules. Clearly labeled bins in the pantry. If everything had a place, if every risk was accounted for, then nothing could spiral. Nothing could disappear.

He stood in his kitchen long after Miles had gone to bed, staring at the neatly lined spice rack he'd reorganized three times in the last month. Cinnamon. Nutmeg. Allspice. Vanilla extract arranged by brand and intensity.

He hated that she'd noticed.

He hated that she'd made him laugh about it.

The house was quiet in that way only houses that have known grief can be. Not peaceful. Not restful. Just… careful. As if the walls themselves were afraid to make noise.

He poured himself a glass of water he didn't want and leaned against the counter, staring out into the dark backyard.

He had not meant to pull back.

That part was important.

He hadn't walked into her bakery intending to retreat. He hadn't touched her jaw intending to flinch away when someone interrupted. He hadn't texted her something dry and distant because he didn't feel something.

He texted it because he felt too much. That was the problem.

Sloane Matthews was chaos. Not reckless chaos — not careless — but alive chaos. Loud. Bright. Sugared and unfiltered. She moved through rooms like she owned them. Like she didn't need permission to exist.

He had forgotten what that looked like.

He had forgotten what it felt like to stand next to someone who wasn't bracing for impact.

The last time he let himself want something without calculating the risk, he'd been standing in a hospital hallway.

The memory hit him without warning — the antiseptic smell, the hum of fluorescent lights, the doctor's voice carefully neutral. He remembered holding a paper cup of vending machine coffee that had gone cold in his hand. He remembered thinking that if he just stood still enough, if he didn't react, the outcome might reverse itself.

It hadn't.

Loss had taught him a simple equation: attachment increases vulnerability.
And vulnerability increases devastation.

So he adapted.

He became measured. Predictable. Structured. A father who double-checked car seat straps and packed balanced lunches and volunteered for PTA oversight committees because oversight meant control.

Control meant safety.

Then Sloane opened a bakery called MILF & Cookies in the middle of Willow Creek and lit a match under everything.

She didn't calculate before she spoke. She didn't moderate herself to make other people comfortable. She didn't pretend to be smaller than she was.

And when she looked at him — not at PTA President Graham Walsh, not at Responsible Widower Graham — but at him, like he was still a man with heat in his chest and not just a role...

He felt exposed.

He had stepped closer in that kitchen. Closer than he'd allowed himself in years. When he touched her jaw, it hadn't been impulsive. It had been deliberate. Reverent, almost. Like he was testing whether something fragile would shatter in his hands.

Then Mindy walked in.

And the room shifted.

He saw the judgment flicker across the space before anyone spoke it. Saw the future headline forming in PTA group chats. Saw the way proximity to Sloane could turn into scrutiny.

He didn't retreat because he was embarrassed of her.

He retreated because he could already see the fallout.

He'd spent years insulating Miles from whispers, from pity, from being "the kid whose mom…" He wasn't willing to expose his son to more instability because he couldn't manage his own pulse.

So he stepped back.

He told himself it was responsible.

He told himself it was temporary.

But when he typed, "Thanks for the cupcakes. Good luck Saturday," he felt the distance in the words. He felt the door closing.

And he hated it.

He set the glass down too hard and exhaled through his nose.

He knew what she'd hear in that text. He knew she was perceptive enough to clock the shift immediately. Sloane didn't miss emotional temperature changes. She lived in them.

She would think he'd changed his mind.

She would think she'd misread him.

She would think she was too much.

That realization sat heavy in his chest.

Because she wasn't too much.

If anything, she was the first person in a long time who made him feel like he wasn't enough.

Not enough life.
Not enough courage.
Not enough willingness to risk something.

He walked down the hallway and paused outside Miles's room. The door was cracked open just slightly. Inside, his son was sprawled across the bed, one arm flung over a half-built Lego spaceship.

Stable.

Safe.

Predictable.

That was his job.

He couldn't afford chaos.

And yet…

He found himself thinking about the way Sloane had looked at her daughter that afternoon. The way Piper believed in her like it was instinct. The way Sloane had stood there absorbing judgment and still managed to smile.

She wasn't unstable.

She was rebuilding.

And there was a difference.

He leaned his forehead briefly against the wall.

He could either keep his distance and watch her harden.

Or he could stand next to her and accept that standing next to fire meant risking heat.

His phone buzzed softly in his hand.

He half-expected a reply from her. Something witty. Something breezy. Something that made it easy for him to pretend he hadn't just chosen fear.

There was nothing.
The silence between them stretched.

For the first time that night, something colder than caution settled in his stomach.

What if she decided he wasn't worth the risk?

What if she chose herself the way he should have chosen her in that room?

He straightened slowly and walked back to the kitchen.

Control had always kept him safe.

But safety had started to feel a lot like loneliness.

And he wasn't sure how much longer he could pretend he preferred it.

chapter seven
The dough will rise

The thing about slow-burn chemistry is that eventually…
it stops burning slow.

It simmers.
It bubbles.
It threatens to boil over on a Tuesday morning while
you're elbow-deep in batter, discussing fundraising
margins, and trying not to imagine what his hands would
feel like under your shirt.

It's subtle.
Until it isn't.

And I'm pretty sure I've sprinted past subtle and into
someone call the fire department, she's about to commit a
sin next to the stand mixer.

Graham Walsh is in my kitchen again. Which sounds
domestic. Cute. Cozy. But Graham didn't come with
"cute."

Graham came with a whiteboard.

And a laser pointer.

"I thought we could map the layout for the bake-off
booths," he says, dead serious, like he's about to brief a
team of Navy SEALs on cupcake strategy.

I stare at the pointer. "Are you planning to give a TED
Talk or direct air traffic?"

He blinks slowly. "This is how I visualize flow."

"This," I tell him, "is how I visualize a restraining order."

He sets the board up anyway, because of course he does.
He holds the pointer like a weapon, draws squares like
he's building a prison, and writes VENDOR FLOW in
block letters that make me want to both admire him and
throw something at his head.

Piper and Miles are in the corner with frosting samples
and a horrifying pile of licorice sticks. They've
constructed what they're calling a Cupcake Coliseum.
Sugarloaf is licking up the casualties.

And I?

I am not okay.

Because Graham—this man with his sleeves rolled and his jaw set and his little concentration frown—has started to feel less like a complication and more like a danger.

Not to my bake-off plan.

To my heart.

To my sanity.

To whatever sliver of control I thought I had left.

He glances over and catches me staring.

"You good?" he asks.

"Fine," I lie. "Just mentally drafting an email to Jesus."

He opens his mouth like he has a response.

And then—he grins.

Not a full grin. Not a charming one. Nothing easy.
But it's real.

A brief crack in the granite and it hits me right between the ribs.

"You're acting weird," he says, pointer still in hand.

I shrug. "You're acting hot. Let's call it even."

He doesn't roll his eyes like he used to. He just goes quiet in a way that makes my skin prickle.

Thoughtful.
Measured.
Like he's weighing risk.

"I'm trying not to ruin this," he says.

I freeze.

54

"Ruin what," I whisper, because my voice suddenly belongs to a different woman. One who's softer. One who's not armored in jokes.

He looks at the whiteboard, then at me.

"This," he says simply. "The event. The committee. The… whatever this is."

My throat tightens.

"Are you afraid of it?" I ask.

"Yes," he says, without hesitation.

Not defensive. Not angry. Just true. It lands like a freight train in a room full of flour.

"Me too," I admit.

The silence that follows isn't awkward. It's heavy. The kind of heavy that makes the air feel thick and close and dangerous.

He steps nearer.

I don't move.

I could.

I *should.*

But my body doesn't want to run from him. My body wants to run to him.

"Tell me to stop," he says softly.

And I should. I should say stop. *Stop. Stop. Stop.* Because I'm a single mom in a small town with a scandalous sign and a fragile heart and I do not need to add "PTA President Romance" to my list of stressors. But instead?

I breathe. And I don't say anything.

His hand brushes my jaw, tentative, like he's not sure I'll let him touch me without turning it into a joke.

And for a second, I don't joke.
For a second, I just… feel.

Then the bakery door slams open like the universe hates romance.

"HELLOOO!" Mindy Clayborn chirps, voice like a chainsaw wrapped in a silk scarf. "Just popping in for a taste test and a quick… chat."

Graham jerks back so fast I'm pretty sure he sprains a moral compass. I swallow the sound in my throat that might've been a laugh or a sob.

"Of course," I say brightly, like I wasn't one breath away from making very poor decisions next to the sour cream. Mindy glides in, clipboard in hand, eyes scanning my counters like she's hunting for mold or sin. Possibly both.

"This looks… festive," she says flatly, picking up a Raspberry Regret Bar with French-tipped talons. "But I do worry about the message you're sending with these names."

I smile sweetly. "The message is: I'm emotionally damaged and talented."

Graham coughs behind me like he's choking on attraction. Mindy's eyes flick to him. Then back to me.

"Some parents," she says, "are concerned it's not a family-friendly image. While no one is suggesting you pull out of the bake-off entirely…"

My stomach drops before she even finishes.

"…there is talk about limiting your role."

The words land like a slap.

Limiting your role.

In other words: You can come, but we'll keep you in your place. I feel old shame rise in my throat like bile. That feeling of being evaluated.

Of being "too much."

Of needing to earn approval I didn't ask for.

Graham goes still beside me. And I know—I know—he wants to say something. I can feel it. But he doesn't. And the silence hurts worse than Mindy's smile.

I laugh, because it's either that or collapse.
"Let me guess," I say. "You'd prefer a wholesome mother who sells banana bread and apologizes for existing."

Mindy's smile tightens. "We'd prefer a representative who doesn't turn every event into a marketing stunt for her midlife crisis."

It hits.

Hard.

The room narrows.

My ears ring.

In the corner, Piper looks up from her frosting chaos, eyes suddenly alert. Like she can sense when grown-ups are being cruel in that socially acceptable way.

Graham's jaw flexes.

But I don't let him speak. Because if he defends me now, I'll want to believe him. And if I believe him, I'll want more. And wanting more is how you end up gutted.

"Well," I say, voice sweet as poison, "lucky for you I've survived worse than PTA gossip."

Mindy pauses just long enough to make it clear she'd like to remind me I'm lucky she's letting me breathe in public. Then she leaves. The bell jingles. The room goes quiet. The whiteboard looks ridiculous now. The laser pointer rests on the counter like an abandoned weapon.

Graham stares at the door.

"That was out of line," he says finally.

I swallow hard. "No."

He turns to me.

"That was the line," I say. "And I knew it was coming. I just hoped… I'd earned more grace than that."

"You have," he says immediately. "From me."

I shake my head, laughter sharp and tired. "That's not how it works. You don't get to see me and then vanish the second it gets real."
His face tightens. He's quiet in that way he gets when he wants to feel something but doesn't know how.

"People like her," he says carefully, "they don't like disruption."

"And I'm disruption," I say.

He looks at me.

"No," he says. "You're… loud life."

The words shouldn't matter.

But they do. Because I've spent years being told I was loud inconvenience.

We don't speak for a moment.

Then Piper yells from the corner, "Mom, Miles glued licorice to Sugarloaf and now she looks like a villain."
Graham exhales a laugh he tries to hide. I cover my face. And somehow, in the middle of humiliation and frosting and judgment…

I feel something shift.

Not comfort.

Not safety.

But resolve.

The dough will rise.

Even if the town wants it flattened.

Later that afternoon, I found Piper and Miles behind the bakery counter whispering like they were planning a bank robbery.

"We're forming a protection committee," Miles informed me.

"For what?" I asked.
"For you," Piper said, serious as a judge.

Miles held up a notebook labeled OPERATION DEFEND MOM.

Inside were bullet points.

• Ignore gossip.
• Collect screenshots.
• Never trust adults who smell like pickles.

I blinked.

"Where did you learn this?" I asked.

Miles shrugged. "My dad reads contracts."

Piper leaned in. "We read vibes."

Chapter Eight
Whispers
SUGAR

The first bad review hit at 6:12 a.m.

Which felt aggressive.

Sloane hadn't even finished frosting the morning batch when Piper came barreling into the kitchen with her iPad.

"Mom," Piper said, eyes wide. "Someone said your cupcakes taste like regret and expired milk."

Sloane blinked slowly.

"That's redundant," she muttered. "Regret already tastes expired."

She wiped her hands on her apron and took the tablet.

The review was one star. No profile photo. No previous reviews.

•••

Username: WillowTruth22
Comment: "Overpriced gimmick bakery pushing alcohol culture to children. Owner unstable. Wouldn't trust her around my family."

•••

Sloane stared at the word unstable longer than the rest.

It sat differently.

Not "tacky."
Not "too much."
Not "inappropriate."

Unstable.

"That's new," she said softly.

"Are we unstable?" Piper asked.

Sloane forced a grin. "Only on Tuesdays."

She handed the tablet back and told Piper to finish her cereal.

Then she checked Yelp.

Three new reviews.

All from accounts created within the last week.

All variations of the same theme.

Gimmick.
Inappropriate.
Irresponsible.
Unstable.

Her jaw tightened.

She'd been in this town long enough to know petty when she saw it.

But this didn't feel petty.

It felt… coordinated.

By ten a.m., she'd received two calls asking whether she served "hard liquor to minors."

By noon, a local mom she barely knew stopped by "just to check" if the cupcakes were properly labeled.

By two, someone had tagged her bakery in a community Facebook group post titled:

"Are We Normalizing This?"

Underneath was a screenshot of her neon sign.

The comments were already spiraling.

"She's clearly going through something."
"This is what happens when we glorify divorce culture."
"Think of the children."

Sloane stared at the thread until her vision blurred.

It was moving too fast.

Way too fast.

She'd expected pushback when she opened.

She hadn't expected strategy.

The bakery was only six months old.

Six months of scraped knuckles and maxed credit cards.
Six months of learning the regulars' orders by heart.
Six months of believing I might actually be allowed to
build something good.

And already they were trying to burn it down.

The bell over the door jingled.

Graham stepped in, clipboard in hand like always.

She didn't look up immediately.

"Did you see the reviews?" she asked.

"Yes."

"And?"

"And I reported the accounts," he said calmly.

She blinked.

"You did?"

"They were created within hours of each other," he
replied. "IP addresses look local."

Her stomach dipped.

"How do you know that?"

He hesitated just slightly. "I asked."

"Asked who?"
"A friend who handles IT for the district."

She stared at him.

"That feels excessive."

He met her gaze. "It feels deliberate."

The word hung between them.

Deliberate.

She swallowed.

"You think this is just… random?"

"No," he said quietly. "I don't."

Silence stretched.

The espresso machine hissed behind her.

Piper laughed in the back room.

The world looked normal.

It didn't feel normal.

Later that afternoon, Sloane found a flyer taped to her window.
It wasn't elaborate. Just black ink on white paper.

"Protect Our Kids."

Underneath:
Say NO to Alcohol-Themed Bakeries Near Schools.

There was no signature.

No group name.

Just implication.
She ripped it down.

Her hands shook.

Not from fear.

From fury.

She marched outside and scanned the square.

A woman across the street pretended to check her phone.

A car idled longer than necessary near the curb.

When Sloane made eye contact with the driver, the car pulled away.

Too quickly.

She stood there for a moment longer than she should have.

Then told herself she was being dramatic.

Small towns bred gossip.

That was all this was.

Right?

That evening, Piper climbed onto a stool at the counter.

"Miss Avery asked about you today," she said casually.

Sloane's hands froze mid-wipe.

"Avery?"

"The nurse," Piper said. "She said she remembers you from before. She asked if you were 'doing better.'"

A slow chill crawled up Sloane's spine.

"Doing better from what?" she asked carefully.

Piper shrugged. "I dunno. She just smiled weird."

Sloane forced a laugh.

"She probably has me confused with someone else."

But something flickered in her memory. Antiseptic.

Fluorescent lights.

A clipboard.

She pressed her fingers to her temples.

The image dissolved before she could grab it.

Stress did that.

She was just stressed.

That night, she checked the bakery locks twice.

Then three times.

The back door stuck slightly when she tested it.

It hadn't done that before.

She told herself wood swelled in humidity.

She told herself she was spiraling.

She told herself she was not unstable.

When she finally crawled into bed, her phone buzzed again.

Another Yelp notification.

Another one-star review.

Another account with no history.
She didn't open it.

Instead, she stared at the ceiling and tried to slow her breathing.

It wasn't the criticism that bothered her.

It was the pattern.

The timing.

The precision.

It felt less like disapproval.

And more like pressure.

Like someone was testing how much she could take.

And for the first time since opening day, the bakery didn't feel like a sanctuary.

It felt like a target.

Chapter Nine
Proofing
the dough
Flour

There are exactly two days until the Willow Creek Winter Bake-Off, and my eyebrows are permanently arched from smiling at people I want to shove into a mixer.

It's amazing how quickly a town decides what kind of woman you are.

Not based on your character.
Not based on your parenting.
Not based on your work ethic.

Based on whether you make them comfortable. And I, unfortunately, am not a comfort person. I'm a "wake up and remember you're alive" person. Which is apparently a crime in Willow Creek.

"Did you hear?" Mindy says at the vendor prep table, sipping a sugar-free latte and dripping judgment like it's an accessory. "They moved your booth to the side entrance. It's just better for crowd control."

I blink slowly.

I nod.

I do not scream. Instead, I pipe frosting onto a test cupcake with such force the bag bursts and sends buttercream across my apron like a dairy explosion of rage.

Piper giggles.

Miles looks horrified.

Graham watches from the other side of the table, scanning a spreadsheet like it's a flotation device.

He doesn't defend me.

He doesn't even look at Mindy.

He just stays Switzerland.

Coward.

"This is sabotage," I whisper to Piper as we restock sample trays. "Passive-aggressive, sparkle-covered sabotage."

Piper shrugs like she's already accepted this is how society functions. "Miss Mindy says she doesn't like your branding strategy."

My jaw tightens. "Did she now."

"She said cupcakes aren't supposed to have cleavage."

That's it.

I am frosting the next PTA meeting into a Hunger Games arena.

Later, Graham and I load supplies for the pre-event vendor walk-through.

The air outside is crisp. The community hall is lit up like a country Pinterest board—burlap banners, string lights, a chalkboard sign that says SWEETEN THE SEASON like we're all in a propaganda video for wholesomeness.

I carry two folding tables while trying not to carry my feelings.

"I'm fine," I say for the third time.

"You're very clearly not fine," Graham mutters, tightening a bungee cord on the sample rack.

"Correct," I snap. "I'm thriving. Nothing says strong female entrepreneur like being body-shamed by a woman in a skort."

He exhales through his nose.

"You could've said something," I add.

His hands still on the cord. "Like what."

"Like... literally anything," I say. "That she's unfair. That she's being cruel. That the bake-off isn't her personal morality pageant."

He's quiet. And that silence lights something in me that's been smoldering since my marriage.

"You're really good at this," I say. "Watching things happen and staying quiet."

His head jerks up. "That's not fair."

I laugh—sharp, humorless. "Neither is being treated like a sideshow because my sign has cleavage energy."

He stares at me like he wants to argue.

Then doesn't.

And I realize:

It's not that he doesn't care. It's that he's terrified of conflict. Or maybe terrified of choosing. Or maybe choosing has cost him before. That thought flickers and vanishes, but it leaves a bruise.

"I made you feel like you saw me," I say quietly. "Like I wasn't just… a joke in this town."

He swallows.

"I do see you," he says.

"But you didn't stand next to me," I whisper.

That lands.

He flinches like I slapped him. He looks away, jaw tight, like he's holding words behind his teeth.

We drive to the hall in silence, the kind that feels like two separate storms trapped in one car.

Outside, vendors set up mock displays. Balloons. Banners. People laughing too loudly. The town pretending everything is wholesome and safe.

Mindy's already there in a blazer that screams Approachable Authority Figure and lip gloss that screams I eat single moms for sport.

"Sloane!" she chirps. "So glad you could make it. We were just reviewing setup flow."

I glance at Graham.

He looks away.

"Perfect," I say flatly. "I'll just be over here, double-checking my offensive signage."

A few PTA moms laugh nervously. Mindy stiffens.

Graham flinches.

I win a small victory I don't even want. Inside, I work alone. I hang string lights. Arrange sample trays. Tape down Piper's hand-drawn sign that says YOU CAN DO IT, MOMMY! with a rainbow made of icing. I stare at it until my throat tightens. Because the truth is: I can do it. I just hate that I have to do it while being watched like a spectacle. And as I step back, I catch my reflection in the glass of the entrance doors.

For a second, behind me, I swear I see a figure near the parking lot.

Still.

Watching.

My skin prickles.

I turn.

No one.

Just cars. Just people. Just lights. I shake it off, but my heart won't settle.

That night, back at the bakery, I'm cleaning until my hands ache when the bell jingles.

Graham steps inside but I don't look at him. He sets down a bag of cocoa powder like it's a peace offering.

"The table doesn't look right without your sign," he says quietly.

I laugh without humor. "Guess I'll have to be less inappropriate moving forward."

He exhales. "I should've said something."

"Yeah," I say. "You should've."

Silence.

Then he speaks like it costs him. "You told me you're scared of failing," he says. "That people think you're too much."

I keep scrubbing.

"Yep," I say. "Good memory."

"I think you're not enough."

My body goes cold. I turn slowly. "Excuse me?"

He steps closer, voice gentler. "You're not enough… for the version of yourself you keep trying to shrink into."

The air leaves my lungs.

He looks wrecked—like he's walking into fire on purpose.

"I don't want you to tone it down," he says. "I just didn't know how to stand next to all that… without getting burned."

My hands shake. "Then leave," I whisper, because it's safer to push than to hope.

He doesn't. He steps closer anyway. "I don't want to leave," he says.

My throat tightens. But I'm tired. Too bruised to keep begging for presence. "So show up," I say. "Or don't come back."

He nods once. Like a vow. Then he walks out.

I stay up late and bake angry. I invent a new cupcake for the bake-off and name it The Midlife Crisis Muffin.

It's tequila, espresso, lime zest, and spite.

Piper finds me passed out on the floor the next morning with icing in my hair and a whisk in my hand.

"You okay, Mommy?" she whispers.

I push myself up, wipe my face, and smile like a woman who's done being shamed.
"I will be," I say.

I have to be. Because tomorrow, I'm showing up. And this time?

I'm not asking permission to exist.

Chapter Ten
Burnt Bridges

Sloane used to think silence was golden.
But this? This silence was glue. Thick. Tacky. Sticking to the roof of her mouth every time she tried to say something — anything — to Graham.

He hadn't said more than six words since they'd left the planning meeting.

The car ride home? A black hole of avoidance.

The text after?

Graham: "Thanks for the cupcakes. Good luck Saturday."

Thanks for the cupcakes?
He might as well have said "Congrats on your funeral."

Thanks for the cupcakes. Good luck Saturday.

It was so neutral. So polite. So professionally distant that it almost impressed her. Graham Walsh could turn emotional retreat into an art form.

Thanks for the cupcakes.

Not I'm sorry I went quiet.
Not About earlier.
Not I didn't mean to freeze when she said that.

Just… cupcakes.

She swallowed.

This was the part where she was supposed to laugh it off.
Make a joke. Send something witty and flirty and light.

Something that made it seem like she hadn't noticed the shift in his tone, the way he'd stepped back like she was something volatile.

But she had noticed.

God, she always noticed.

Her thumb hovered over the keyboard. She could feel the familiar pull — the urge to fix it. To soften it. To perform her way back into warmth.

No worries! Can't wait! Bring your clipboard!

That was the old version of her. The version who smoothed edges. The version who pretended everything was fine so no one had to sit in discomfort.

But what if everything wasn't fine?

What if that almost-kiss had been a mistake in his eyes? What if the look she thought she saw — the one that felt like hunger, like recognition — had just been proximity and sugar and wishful thinking?

Maybe she imagined it. Maybe she always imagined it.

Her chest tightened. She hated this part. The part where doubt crept in and started rearranging the story she'd told herself.

A week ago, she would've sworn he wanted her. Not just physically — though that had been obvious in the way his jaw tightened when she teased him — but emotionally. Like he saw her. Like he understood that the loudness was armor. That the flirtation was strategy. That the humor was scaffolding holding up something fragile.

But now? Now he was back behind glass. And maybe that was the truth.

Maybe he had stepped closer and realized what everyone eventually did — that being near her was exciting in theory, exhausting in practice.

She replayed the last few weeks in her mind like security footage.

The whiteboard.
The flour-dusted fingers brushing.
The way his voice dropped when he said he didn't want to ruin this.
The way he looked at her like she was something he hadn't let himself want in a long time.

Had she leaned in too fast? Had she made it too big? She exhaled slowly and leaned back against the kitchen counter, phone still glowing in her hand.

This is what she did. She burned things before they were done. She mistook warmth for permanence. She built castles out of glances and then acted surprised when they collapsed.

Her ex had said it once, in that low, tired voice that meant he'd already checked out.
"You make everything intense, Sloane. It doesn't have to be that deep."

She used to think he meant she cared too much. Now she wondered if he meant she was too much. The text felt like confirmation.

Good luck Saturday.

Good luck alone.

Her stomach twisted.

She hated how quickly she could spiral from hopeful to humiliated. How easily she could go from bold and unapologetic to questioning every word she'd said, every look she'd misread.

Maybe Graham hadn't pulled back because he was scared.

Maybe he pulled back because he finally saw the full picture — messy, loud, frosting-stained, emotionally high-maintenance — and decided he didn't want to sign up for it.

Maybe he deserved better.

The words from the bathroom replayed in her head even though they hadn't happened yet — that imagined chorus of women who always seemed to be just one whisper ahead of her.

Someone like him? He deserves stability.

She pressed her lips together.

Stability.

She tried the word on like a coat that didn't fit. She wasn't unstable. She was rebuilding.

There was a difference… Wasn't there?

She stared down at the message again.

Thanks for the cupcakes.

She wanted to throw her phone across the room.

Instead, she set it down gently.

Because somewhere, deep down, beneath the sarcasm and the sugar and the bravado, there was a smaller voice asking something much quieter.

What if he's right to hesitate? What if this town is right? What if I am just… too loud for someone who's already survived loss?

The thought lodged in her chest like a splinter.

She had fought so hard not to shrink again. And now here she was — shrinking preemptively, just in case.

Her thumb hovered over the keyboard one more time.

She typed three words.

No problem. Thanks.

Then deleted them. Then typed nothing at all.

She set the phone face down.

If he wanted distance, she could give him distance. She was good at distance. She'd lived inside it for years.

But as she stood there in the quiet kitchen, surrounded by sugar and stainless steel and a life she'd built with trembling hands, one truth settled heavy in her stomach:

It didn't hurt because he rejected her.

It hurt because she almost believed she wasn't alone anymore.

And that was far more dangerous.

Back at the bakery, Sloane pulled out a mixing bowl like it was body armor. She beat sugar and eggs like they'd personally offended her. Her arms ached from whisking by hand — she needed to feel something.

But no amount of cracked eggshells or whipped batter could make her feel clean again.

She felt… rejected. Like she was too much. Again.
The worst part?

It wasn't that Graham didn't want her.
It was that he almost did.

The way he'd looked at her a week ago — fingers brushing against hers over spilled flour, soft smile tugging at the edge of his mouth, like maybe, just maybe, he was ready to want something messy — something real.

And now?

Gone.

The doorbell jingled and in walked Satan in blush pink linen, aka Mindy, flanked by two PTA moms who never wore anything under a $75 price tag or over a size six.

"Oh wow," Mindy chirped, eyes wide as she surveyed the half-decorated bakery. "You're really… going for it."

Sloane wiped her hands on her apron and pasted on her best Southern smile. "You bet. Nothing like stress-baking until your joints lock up."

"I just didn't realize you'd still be competing," Mindy said, voice syrupy. "After… you know."

Sloane blinked. "After what?"

A flicker of fake innocence. "Oh, didn't you hear? The booth rearrangement. They moved you to the back near the service entrance."

Sloane felt the air leave the room.

"But don't worry," Mindy added. "We all admire how resilient you are. Really. Trying so hard to… stay relevant."

One of the other women snorted.

Sloane's hand curled around a frosting spatula like it was a weapon.

"Thanks," she said. "That means a lot coming from a woman who coordinates snack duty with Botox appointments."

They left in a flurry of thin laughter and Chanel perfume.

Sloane stood still.

Then grabbed the tray of cupcake samples she'd been prepping and hurled it into the trash.

She didn't cry.
Not yet.
Not until she locked the doors and turned off the lights.

The next morning, Piper found her asleep on the bakery floor, curled up in a blanket of flour and regret.

"Are you sick?" Piper asked.

Sloane smiled. "A little."

"Do you still love baking?"

Sloane paused. "I think I do. I just don't love feeling like a joke."

Piper handed her a drawing: a cupcake with a crown and angry eyebrows.

"This is you," she said. "Queen Cupcake. You always win. Even when people are mean."

Sloane bit her lip.

Her daughter was seven.

And somehow, the only adult in the room.

By that afternoon, she was back on her feet, pretending like the frosting-covered breakdown never happened.

She delivered samples. She fixed the booth signage. She even called the fire marshal to make sure her booth still met code — even if it was stuck in the back like a shameful secret.

She was keeping it together.

Until the PTA Happy Hour.

Graham wasn't there.
Which should've made it easier. But it didn't.

Instead, it left her exposed — raw in a sea of perfect ponytails and airbrushed smiles.

She sipped a watered-down wine spritzer and tried to look normal.

Then it happened.

Two moms. One bathroom.
She hadn't meant to eavesdrop — but they didn't notice her washing her hands in the far stall.

"I heard he ended things."

"Can you blame him? She's a mess."

"Honestly, someone like him? He deserves better. Stability. Not some chaotic bakery divorcee with frosting in her hair and feelings all over the place."

Laughter.

The kind that cuts.

She waited until they left.

Then stood in front of the mirror, mascara smudged, lip gloss faded, and wondered when exactly she became the villain in her own love story.

She didn't go home.

She went to the bakery.
Alone.

She turned off the lights. Sat in the middle of the floor.

And stared at the framed certificate from the day she opened: "MILF & COOKIES: Willow Creek's Booziest Bakery."

She'd been so proud.
She'd believed she could build something from the ashes
of a life that had crumbled.

And now? Now she wasn't sure

She sat alone with the memory of meeting her shoppe for
the first time. The bakery had smelled like lemon bleach
and wet wood the first time Sloane walked in.

The "For Lease" sign was crooked in the window, the
paint was chipped, and someone had left half a muffin
fossilized on the counter. It was nothing like she
imagined.

And still—
She cried.

Not big, dramatic sobs.
Just one stupid, stinging tear that slipped down her cheek
and landed on the peeling vinyl floor.

Because the moment she stepped inside, she saw it.

Not what it was. But, what it could be.

There, by the window? A sunlit table for two, always
dusted with powdered sugar.
The counter? Rebuilt with reclaimed wood, lined with
glittering bottles of bourbon and cinnamon whiskey.
And behind it?
Her.
Not the wife of a man who needed her smaller. Not the
mom who'd fallen apart.

Just Sloane.
Rebuilt from scratch.

"I'll take it," she'd told the realtor, before she had a business plan or a clue.

He blinked. "Don't you want to—uh, sit with it?"

"No," she said. "If I sit, I'll talk myself out of it."

She didn't sit.

She didn't breathe, either, for about three months.
She maxed out a credit card on reclaimed bar stools. She painted the walls a color called "Buttered Rum" while Piper napped on a comforter in the corner. She cried over burnt simple syrup and watched YouTube tutorials on how to soundproof a commercial kitchen.

Her hands were always sticky. Her feet always hurt. Her voice went hoarse from smiling too hard at city inspectors.

But every night she locked the door and looked back at the display case—

—empty, but clean.

And thought: I'm doing it. I'm building something.
Not perfect. Not safe.
But hers.

It wasn't until weeks later, when she finally opened the doors, that she realized what she'd really built:

A place to belong.

For people like her — messy, loud, flawed, too much.
People who loved sweet things with a splash of something stronger.

She hung a sign in the window that said:

"Life's a hot mess. Might as well frost it."

And for the first time in a long time, she felt something close to whole.

She pulled out her phone and began to draft a message:

"I'm pulling out of the bake-off. Sorry to disappoint. I'm just… not who I thought I was."

Then she stared at the send button.

She didn't press it.

But she also didn't delete it.

Instead, she curled up on the bench seat behind the counter, surrounded by flour and tequila extract and a list of everything she hadn't done right.
The bench behind the counter had become her unofficial bed. She didn't mean to sleep there again. But it felt safer than going home. Or worse — pretending she wasn't unraveling.

The glow from the EXIT sign cast a red shadow across the bakery. It looked like a warning.

She rolled over and saw it — the certificate. The one from opening day.
It was still a little crooked in the frame.

And just like that, she was back there.

The bakery had still smelled like lemon bleach and wet wood the first time she stepped inside. "For Lease" sign barely hanging. Cracked tiles. Not a single ounce of charm.

But it had been quiet.

And Sloane had needed quiet.
After the lawyers. After the custody schedule. After the text that read "She's just easier."

This space was blank. And blank was better than broken.

When the realtor handed her the key, he said, "You sure?" She'd nodded so hard her teeth hurt. "Nope."

He laughed.
She didn't.

She painted every wall herself. Built the menu with Sharpie and hope. Piper colored cupcake mascots in crayon at the counter. They ate dinner on upturned milk crates and celebrated with store-brand cider.

She burned the first five batches of anything. Used the wrong salt twice. Flooded the sink.

But she kept showing up. Even when nobody else did. Because this place? This was hers. And now? It felt like a paper doll house soaked in shame.

She sat up on the bench, rubbing her face. Her skin felt like it didn't belong to her.

She opened her phone again. Stared at the unsent text. "I'm pulling out of the bake-off. Sorry to disappoint. I'm just... not who I thought I was."

I was six months pregnant and too tired to fight anyone when the divorce papers came. That's the part people don't see.

They see the neon sign. The bourbon cupcakes. The sharp mouth.

They don't see me in a courthouse bathroom, hands braced against the sink, swollen ankles and mascara running, trying to convince myself that raising a child alone wasn't the worst thing that could happen.

I signed papers with one hand and held my stomach with the other. Piper kicked the entire time. Like she already knew she was going to be my reason. For seven years, I did it alone. Not tragically. Not heroically. Just… quietly.

And maybe that's why this hurt so much.

Because I built this bakery the same way I built my life after him.

From scratch.
From fear.
From exhaustion.

And I will not let someone reduce it to a punchline.

She stared at it. And then hit save again without sending it.

Outside, the sun was coming up. But everything felt darker.

She checked the bakery voicemail and paused.

One new message.

Mindy's voice.
Chipper. Plastic.

"Hey Sloane! Just a heads up that your delivery slot for Saturday moved to 5:45 a.m. They said you missed the final vendor call. Sorry you didn't get the memo! Hope that doesn't throw off your prep!"

She didn't scream.
Didn't throw her phone.

She just sat.
Silent. Still.

Then she opened Yelp and typed "bakery for sale near me."

She didn't press enter. But this time, she didn't close the tab either.

CHAPTER ELEVEN

The rain began like a rumor and turned into a storm.

It needled the front windows of the bakery, traced trembling lines down the glass, pooled at the curb in a small, impatient river. Inside, the hum of the refrigerators and the smell of sugar felt wrong—too bright, too cheery on a night that had the color of old bruise.

Sloane sat on the stainless counter with one shoe off and one still on, both useless. She'd let her hair down and forgotten about it; now it hung in damp ropes that smelled like vanilla and rain and the little panic she'd swallowed all afternoon. The laptop glowed on the prep table. The tab she shouldn't have opened—Bakeries For Sale—still stared back at her like a dare.

"Shut up," she whispered to it, and took another sip of whiskey.

The bourbon wasn't good. It was what was left—sharp at the back of the throat, mean on the way down—and she took it anyway, because grief was a terrible thing to carry sober.

Sugarloaf thumped his tail lazily against the mat by the door and sighed like a disapproving grandparent. She raised her glass in his direction.

"To terrible ideas," she said, and the bell over the door jingled.

"We're closed," she said, without looking up.

"I brought coffee," said a low voice.

The name hit her body before it hit her ears. Her spine went hot and cold and stubbornly straight. She blinked at the laptop screen until the letters blurred, then slid off the counter and turned.

Graham stood in the doorway with his shoulders wet and his sleeves shoved up and his hair darkened by rain. He looked like a man halfway between decisions. He held two cups in one hand and regret in the other.

"You can't be here," she said, and immediately wanted to swallow it back. It sounded like a dare. It sounded like she wanted him to come closer. She did. She didn't.

He stepped inside and let the door sigh shut behind him. The bell chimed again, small and earnest.
"You weren't answering your phone," he said. "Miles said Piper said you were… not okay."

"We don't use that language here," she said lightly. "We say 'medium-rare meltdown.'"

A flicker tugged at the corner of his mouth, then vanished. He held out a cup, unsure. "Oat milk. No syrup." He remembered. Of course he remembered.

She took it because not taking it would be a different kind of confession. The coffee was too hot and exactly right. It made the rain sound farther away.

"So," she said, staring into the steam, "which is it tonight? PTA President or drive-by pessimist?"

"Neither," he said. "Just me."

"Mm," she said. "That one's new."

He flinched but didn't retreat. He took in the empty case, the scattered trays, the laptop, the tab. She watched him see it all, piece by careful piece, like he was assembling the proof of a crime.

"You're not selling," he said quietly.

"Who said selling?" she said. "Browsing. Flirting. Window shopping my future failure. It's very chic."

The muscle in his jaw worked. "Don't," he said.

"Don't what?"

"Talk about yourself like that." He blew out a breath that sounded like a confession fleeing. "Don't… make jokes to keep me from hearing you."

She laughed, sharp. "That's rich, coming from the man who communicates entirely in spreadsheets and evasive eye contact."

The rain pressed harder. Somewhere in the back, a timer blinked 00:00 in red, insistent and useless.

He moved closer, careful like approaching a stray cat, and stopped at the edge of the counter as if some invisible line had been drawn there and he'd promised himself he wouldn't cross it.

"I heard what Mindy said at happy hour," he said. "I should've shut it down. I should've—" His mouth flattened. "I didn't."

"No," she said. "You didn't."

"I'm sorry."

"Are you?" She lifted the coffee, set it down, picked up the whiskey. "Because I can't do anything with that. With 'sorry.' It just… sits there. Like a wet napkin."

His eyes flicked to the whiskey, to the laptop, back to her face. "Why the tab?"

She swallowed. The answer pooled in her mouth like something heavy and sweet and hard to say. "I don't want to be funny anymore," she said. "Not like this. Not because I'm defending myself for existing."

He stared at her. She felt naked, and not in the glittery, powerful way—naked like the truth was showing through a dress she hadn't realized was sheer.

"Sloane," he said softly.

"Don't," she said again, because she knew that voice. It had been in his texts, beneath the dutiful, beneath the brave. A secret voice. A dangerous one.

He took a breath, steadied it with visible effort, and put both hands flat on the counter. Not touching her. Close enough that she could feel the warmth of him through the metal. "I pulled back," he said. "Because I'm a coward. Because wanting anything scares me. Because whenever I let myself… I lose it."

"Your wife," she said, and the word felt like a prayer they weren't allowed to say.

He nodded. "And the life I understood. The rules. I have lived inside rules for so long I mistook them for safety."

Her throat burned. "And me?"

"You are not safe," he said, and it should have sounded like an indictment. It didn't. It sounded like awe. "You laugh too loud. You cry in your own kitchen. You name pastries like confessions and then tell the truth with frosting. You terrify me."

"Okay," she said, and her voice shook. "And?"

"And I want you anyway."

Something in her ribcage buckled. She tried to hold onto the counter and realized she'd grabbed his wrist. Felt his pulse kick under her thumb. Let go like it burned and then, traitorously, sought it again.

"I don't know how to be wanted without being performed," she said. The admission dragged itself out of her by the hair. "I don't know how to be loved without auditioning for it."

"You don't have to audition with me," he said. "You can be… wrong. Messy. Loud. Quiet. You can be cruel on bad days and gentle on worse ones. You can have nothing left to give and still be enough."

She let out a sound that wasn't a laugh and wasn't a sob. "Don't say pretty things to me in storms," she whispered. "I'll believe them."

"Good," he said. "Believe them."

He was breathing a little faster now, like the distance between honesty and touch was a hill he didn't trust his own feet on. "I won't ask you to forgive me for the last week," he said. "I didn't deserve you in it."

"And today?" she asked. "Do you deserve me today?"

His eyes found hers and held. "I am trying to."

The words landed in her bones, warm and steadying, like a hand between her shoulder blades saying forward, go on, I won't let you fall.

She reached up to tuck a damp piece of hair behind her ear and her fingers shook. She looked at them like they belonged to a stranger, then set the whiskey aside, then the coffee. Empty hands. Nowhere to hide.

"Come here," she said, and when he didn't immediately move, she added, quieter, "Please."

He crossed the small distance like it was time instead of space. Up close he smelled like wet wool and rain and the particular clean of him, the one that had haunted the necklines of her daydreams. He was careful and she was not. She hooked her fingers in his shirt and let herself pull, and he let himself be pulled, and when his forehead touched hers the whole noisy day fell briefly, beautifully silent.

"I'm mad at you," she said into the breath between them.

"I know," he murmured. "Be mad at me and still let me hold you."

And so she did.

His hands came around her like a promise he had practiced but never spoken aloud. Not possessive— anchoring. He was warm everywhere she was cold. Steady everywhere she trembled. The first kiss wasn't a kiss, not really—more a press, a question, a yes if you want it. She did. God, she did.

"Again," she said, and he did, and this time it was something that had lived between them since the first argument in the pantry—sweet and sharp and a little stunned to find itself finally allowed.

She tasted rain on him. He tasted bourbon on her. Somewhere in the back, the old fridge kicked on and the sound made her laugh into his mouth. He smiled, and it broke her in a gentle way.

"This is a terrible idea," she said, because she always said that when she meant this is a true thing and I'm scared.

"We've had worse," he said, and kissed her like he was done choosing fear.

When they parted, the room felt changed, as if someone had opened a window. They didn't rush to fill the quiet. They let it hover, bright and uncertain, like a newly risen soufflé.

He rested his temple against hers. "Tell me you're not selling," he said. It was almost childlike, that hope. She could hear the careful man in it, building a bridge in his own head plank by plank.

"I'm not pressing enter tonight," she said. "That's the best I can give you right now."

"It's enough."

"It might not be tomorrow."

"Then I'll come back tomorrow," he said, as if it were that simple, and maybe—with him choosing—it could be.

A timer she hadn't set began to beep in the dark kitchen. Some old alarm left on from the afternoon. Sloane snorted, swiped at her eyes with the heel of her hand, and slid off the counter. He stepped back just enough to let her pass and then followed her through the swinging door like he belonged in her wake.
They stood shoulder to shoulder in the small square of fluorescent light, staring at nothing that needed saving. She turned the timer off. The silence crept back, less sharp this time.

"Stay," she said, surprising herself with the word. "Not —" she flapped a hand, heat climbing her neck "—not like stay-stay. Just… don't make me be brave alone for an hour."

"Okay," he said. "I can do an hour."

They tried to make coffee and failed and laughed about it in whispers as if the night were a sleeping child. She found a mixing bowl and the last of the good chocolate and set out to make the whiskey truffles she'd ruined the first week they opened—the ones she always made when she needed to remember that you could scorch a thing and still coax sweetness from it.

He grated chocolate while she warmed the cream. Their elbows bumped. Their hands did, too. Every small touch was a spark that didn't demand to be a fire.

"Why truffles?" he asked.

"Because they start as a collapse," she said, tipping the cream into the chopped chocolate. "You pour the heat in and everything falls apart into something ugly and glossy and impossible. And then—if you keep stirring, if you don't flinch—you get silk. You get what you were hoping for but couldn't see at the start."

He watched the mixture go from broken to smooth. "Is this a metaphor?" he asked softly.

"Everything is, with me," she said, and it wasn't self-mockery this time. It was just the map of who she was. They let the ganache rest. They leaned on opposite sides of the prep table and told each other small things that fit in the space between midnight and morning.

He told her Miles had started humming while he did homework; he didn't know when it had begun, only that the house felt different with sound in it. She told him Piper had named the mixer "Beyoncé" because it worked harder than everyone and still looked good under lights. He told her he'd thrown a punch once, years ago, and had never stopped being embarrassed by the satisfaction it gave him. She told him she'd once driven to the beach at three a.m. in a storm and screamed herself hoarse into the dark because there was nothing left to do but choose herself and drive back.

"Do you ever think you'll stop being angry at Mindy?" he asked finally.

"Not tonight," she said. "Maybe not for a while. But anger's just grief in heels. It doesn't run as fast as it thinks it does."

He huffed a laugh that sounded like it had been waiting a long time to be let out.
When the ganache was ready, she scooped and rolled and dusted, and he made himself useful, clumsy and earnest and entirely present. Truffles lined up like small dark moons. She slipped one between her lips and closed her eyes. Heat, bitterness, sugar. When she opened them, he was watching her like an answer he hadn't dared write down.

"Here," she said, and held one out. He took it from her fingers and didn't look away while it melted. The air snapped. Neither moved closer. Neither moved away.

"We're going to be so stupid tomorrow," she said, grinning helplessly.

"We were stupid yesterday," he said. "Tonight we're just honest."

The clock over the back door ticked in polite, reasonable seconds. The rain softened.

He pulled his phone from his pocket like a man remembering something and winced. "I need to text Miles. He's at my sister's and I told him I was… running an errand."

"What errand is this, exactly?" she asked.

"The important kind," he said, thumbs moving. "The one you don't name until you're sure you didn't ruin it."

She watched him send whatever he sent, the little frown of concentration, the way his shoulders eased when the dots appeared. She wanted to memorize ridiculous things about him: the way he tapped the side of the phone twice before putting it down, the way he always looked at a door before he left a room, the rasp that lived in his voice when he was tired.

When he set the phone aside, he looked at her like someone preparing to ask a question that could change the shape of the night. Her heart did a clumsy thing against her sternum.

"Don't propose," she said lightly. "I already have a frosting ring."

"Marry me to your chaos," he said anyway, soft, a smile buried in it.

She tipped her head back and laughed until her eyes watered. "God, you're dangerous when you try."
"I'm trying," he said again, no humor in it this time. "I'll keep trying."

A small, sane voice in her head—one that sounded annoyingly like her mother—reminded her that trying wasn't a contract and words were wind. But the way he looked at her wasn't wind. It was brick and mortar and a door he'd left open.

She nodded. "Then come to the bake-off tomorrow and take my side in public."

"Done."

"Even if I name a tart something unholy."

"Especially then."

"Even if your friends look at you like you're crazy."

"They already do."

"Even if I… lose?" The word slipped out, uninvited. She hated it. She hated that she cared.

He stepped around the table until they were close enough that their breath remembered what to do with each other. "I don't care about the trophy," he said. "I care about you walking in there like the room belongs to you."

Her face crumpled for a second, just long enough to show before she steadied it. "It doesn't."

"It will," he said simply. "Because you'll be in it."

She reached for him again without asking permission from the committee in her head. The kiss that followed wasn't urgent; it was the opposite—patient and precise, a slow proofing of a dough that needed time. His hand found the small of her back and the world aligned in one quiet click.

When they parted, she pressed her forehead to his collarbone and listened to the steady, unshowy drum of his heart. The safest metronome she had known in years.

"Stay until the rain stops," she murmured.

"I'll stay until you tell me to go," he said, and she didn't.

They cleaned up without making it about the future. He put chairs on tables. She labeled a tray she hadn't believed in an hour ago. He bent to scratch Sugarloaf until the dog rolled over in ecstasy and exposed the frosting eyeball still stuck to his tail. They both grinned like children and neither apologized for it.

At the door, he hesitated. It wasn't a dramatic pause. It was small, human. "If you panic tomorrow," he said, "look for me."

"What if you panic?"

"Then I'll look for you."

She nodded as if they'd agreed on a weather report and not a pact.

"Goodnight, Sloane."

"Goodnight, Graham."

He stepped into the soft, lingering drizzle and pulled the door gently until the bell gave a single, sweet chime. She stood there for a moment, palm on the cool glass, and watched his shape blur and vanish into the rain.

The bakery was quiet again. Not wrong this time—expectant.

She moved to the laptop. The tab still waited, bright and cruel. She hovered, then closed it. The sudden dark of the screen made the room feel larger.

On the counter, her phone buzzed.

A text from Graham:

G: Don't forget—your booth doesn't live in the back. You do. See you front and center.

She didn't write back. She didn't have to. She looked around at the empty case and the trays and the crooked certificate and the life she had built that was messy and loud and exactly hers, and she let herself want it again.

"Okay," she said to the room, to herself, to the storm that had finally softened into a hush. "Okay."

She turned the OPEN sign off and left the lights on, just for tonight, like a lighthouse you could eat your way toward. Then she went to the back to find the good ribbon Piper insisted they use for "lucky bows," and somewhere between the shelf and the sink she realized she was humming.

It wasn't a song she knew.

But it sounded like staying.

CHAPTER TWELVE

Morning arrived soft and gold, like the town had forgiven the night for being heavy.

Sloane braided her hair the way Piper liked—loose and messy, with a red ribbon threaded through like a promise —and tied on the apron that said BAKE ME HARDER because she refused to apologize for surviving with style. She iced a last test shortcake, tasted the glaze—just enough bite to make you pay attention—and told the mirror, "Front and center."

Piper popped into the bathroom with glitter on her eyelashes and a serious expression. "Queen Cupcake," she said, hands on hips, "today we take no prisoners."

"Only trophies," Sloane said, and kissed her forehead.

They loaded the van. Graham texted once, a simple: Front. Center. I've got you. – G

The message slotted into her chest like a missing brick.

The town square already buzzed when they arrived— white tents like little clouds, tables skirted in cheerful gingham, a brass band warming up on the gazebo. The air smelled like cinnamon and fried dough and that specific kind of optimism small towns reserve for festivals and parades. Mindy was there in a cream blazer that dared ketchup to touch it. She wore a volunteer badge with too many ribbons. She was a walking spreadsheet.

"Sloane!" she trilled, voice sweet with a lemon twist. "You must've missed my message. Your booth is—"

"Here," Graham said, appearing at Sloane's shoulder like he'd been conjured. He wore a navy button-down rolled to the elbows and the expression of a man who'd chosen a hill to die on. He held a laminated map and pointed to the prime spot in front of the gazebo. A placard read: MILF & Cookies — Featured Vendor.

Mindy blinked. "That area is for vendors we're… confident about."

"That's us," Sloane said, too brightly. "Confidently inappropriate."

Graham didn't look away from Mindy. "Principal Navarro approved the change last night. We're highlighting small business owners who donated additional inventory to the kids' tasting table." He raised a brow. "Sloane did."

Mindy's smile tightened until it looked expensive. "Of course," she said through her teeth. "Front and center, then."

"Front and center," Sloane echoed, and tried not to visibly lean into Graham's warmth.

He didn't touch her. He didn't have to. The town watched the way they stood near each other and drew their own conclusions.

Good. They worked. Sloane fell into the choreography she'd built for herself—the one that made chaos look like charm.

Piper arranged the signage she'd drawn: SPIKED STRAWBERRY SHORTCAKE WITH HAPPY ENDING GLAZE in rainbow bubble letters. Miles, grave with purpose, placed tiny cards that listed allergens and a footnote that read ADULTS ONLY (SORRY, KIDS— HAVE A "BEHAVE-YOURSELF BERRY CUP" INSTEAD).

"Is 'Happy Ending' a massage thing?" asked a dad who should've known better.

"It's a baking thing," Sloane said sweetly. "Like when your cake rises even though you forgot to pray."

Laughter rippled. Mindy inhaled sharply, like someone had scratched her pearl coating.

The band struck up "Uptown Funk." Sugarloaf—on a short leash tied to the leg of the tent—wagged his frosting eyeball tail like an accessory.

"Ready?" Graham asked quietly, sidling up to Sloane with a clipboard he probably didn't need. The gray at his temples made him look expensive and ruinable.

"Born," Sloane said, and smoothed a hand down her apron.

He watched her hand, then her face. "You're luminous."

"Say it louder into the PA," she said, because when she was shy she doubled down on bravado. He smiled anyway, like he heard the tremor beneath. The first wave hit hard—strollers, tween girls, men with craft coffee and opinions. The "Happy Ending" line doubled back on itself in five minutes. Sloane moved like fight and art—slice, dollop, drizzle, crown with macerated strawberries, pass with a wink. Piper perfected a flourish. Miles said, "Please enjoy responsibly" to anyone who looked like a liability, which was everyone.

Graham did crowd control as if he'd been born for it— polite, unyielding, strangely charming when he said "one per wristband, ma'am" to a woman who could buy the town.

"This glaze is… complex," said a food-blogger type with a DSLR and a ring light.

"It's a second chance in sauce form," Sloane said. "Start sweet. End brave."

The blogger blinked like she'd been given a plot twist. "I love a narrative dessert."

"Same," Sloane said, and kept moving.

The ex showed up at noon. Of course he did.

He wore that tech-bro relaxed wealth uniform—sneakers too clean, smile too practiced. Beside him: New Girlfriend, younger and nervously pretty, trying to look like she'd always belonged to this town. She studied the booth like it was a test.

Sloane's stomach did an old, stupid dip. Then it steadied.

She didn't owe the past any more of her posture.

"Hey," the ex said, like he'd found a quarter. "This is… popular."

"People like joy," Sloane said. "It's catching."

New Girlfriend's voice was breathy but earnest. "I follow your Instagram. Your captions are… unhinged." She flushed. "In a good way."

"Thanks," Sloane said. "They're written by a committee in my head. We vote. Chaos wins."

The ex offered a small smile. "Proud of you."

The words were cheap; they had the weight of lint. Sloane nodded anyway and cut two samples, slid them across the table, and looked only at the woman.
"I hope he treats you better than he treated me," she said pleasantly. "And if he doesn't, come by on Thursdays. We do 'Dump Him' Danish." She smiled. "Two for one."

New Girlfriend startled, then laughed—a startled, grateful sound. The ex shifted, chastened. Sloane handed over the plates. "Enjoy," she said. "No returns."

Graham materialized to stand at her side like a nonverbal boundary. He offered the ex a neutral nod that somehow felt like a line in the sand.

Sloane didn't need rescuing. But she liked being… backed.

They moved on.

"Attention!" Mindy sang into the microphone from the gazebo. "We'll begin judging the FEATURED VENDOR category in fifteen minutes. Please make your case to the judges clearly and concisely—no theatrics." She looked directly at Sloane when she said it.

"Did she just subtweet me in person?" Sloane muttered.

Piper tugged her sleeve. "Time for your speech."

"I don't have a speech."

"That's your superpower," Graham said. "You have a truth."

She rolled her shoulders back until they felt like they lived on her body again. "Okay," she said. "Truth it is."

The judges approached in a decorative cluster—Principal Navarro leading with a clipboard, Mindy with a smile like a locked door, and a visiting pastry chef from the next county wearing a scarf that screamed AUTHORITY.

Sloane greeted them with steady hands and a ribbon-bright grin. She placed three perfect plates on a tasting board like she was laying down a hand of cards.

"Spiked Strawberry Shortcake with a Happy Ending Glaze," she said. "The strawberries are macerated in lemon and a whisper of Cointreau. The shortcake is butter-heavy and unapologetic. The glaze has a crack of black pepper and a good splash of Prosecco." She looked at Navarro and then at the kids gathered behind him. "The tasting cups on the left are alcohol-free—same joy, less drama."

Mindy sniffed. "And the name is family-friendly… how?"

"It's about finishing strong," Sloane said, and let the beat breathe. "In baking. And in life."

A laugh moved through the crowd. One judge tried to hide a smile behind a spoon.

Sloane went on. She didn't read the speech she didn't write. She just told the truth.

"I named this because I started this bakery at the end of something. The ending was messy and humiliating and loud. But I found out endings can be sweet, too, if you put enough love into what comes next—if you learn to let the heat do its work and then trust yourself not to flinch."

She met Mindy's eyes. Didn't look away.

"And yes," she added warmly, "sometimes I'm too much. Lucky me."

A small cheer cracked open and spread. Navarro blinked quickly like he had dust in his eye.

The pastry chef took a slow bite, closed her eyes, and then —deadpan—said, "I would ruin my life for this glaze."

The crowd laughed. Sloane felt her knees threaten to go and planted her feet harder.

Mindy recovered. "Thank you," she said crisply. "We'll —"

A voice called from beside the gazebo. New Girlfriend again—cheeks pink, courage summoned. "I don't know the rules," she said, "but I know I've never seen this many happy people in one line." She gestured to the mass of locals waiting patiently, laughing, trying to sneak seconds. "That seems like a vote."

Mindy's smile cracked like candy pulled too thin.

Graham stepped forward—not touching Sloane, but anchoring her with his voice. "For the record," he said into the PA Navarro offered him, "the PTA thanks MILF & Cookies for donating an extra 150 kids' tastings and for helping design the allergy labeling that every vendor is using today. That's leadership. That's community." He looked at Sloane like the word belonged to her. "That's front and center."

It landed. You could feel the town decide.

Awards time was a blur. There were ribbons and applause and Piper's hand gripping Sloane's like a lifeline.
Someone fainted—actually fainted—when Navarro announced Featured Vendor:
MILF & Cookies and Sugarloaf howled on an unhelpful note of triumph. Mindy smiled like a brittle ornament and clapped because it was structurally required.

Sloane accepted the ribbon with a smile that felt like oxygen finally arriving. She bent to whisper to Piper, "We did it," and Piper whispered back, "You did it," and then added, "Now kiss him."

"Subtle," Sloane said, and turned.

Graham was already there. Not too close. Not claiming. Just… choosing. In front of everyone.

"You were impossible," he said quietly, reverently. "In the best way."

She laughed, helpless and bright. "You're about to be in so many emails."

"Worth it," he said, and then—because the town had already made up its mind and she had made up hers—she put a hand on his chest and brought his mouth to hers. It wasn't a movie kiss. It was a promise. The kind you make when the worst parts of you have already shaken hands and agreed to try anyway. It tasted like strawberries and relief and the kind of future you earn in small, stubborn inches.

The crowd erupted. Someone wolf-whistled. The brass band, chaotic and perfect, launched into an upbeat march like a soundtrack that had been waiting for its cue.

Sloane pulled back, a little breathless and a lot alive. "Hi," she said, like they were starting for real now.

"Hi," he said, and his smile slipped crooked with something that looked a lot like peace.

Behind them, Piper and Miles did a solemn fist bump as if they had orchestrated the entire arc from day one.

Mindy approached with the ribbon, chin high, mouth polite. "Congratulations," she said to Sloane, and then— so quiet it barely counted as speech—"And for what it's worth… that tart name is clever."

Sloane blinked. "Is that… friendship?"

Mindy's lips twitched. "It's détente. Don't push it."

"Never," Sloane said, already plotting a 'Detente Donut' for Tuesday.

By late afternoon, the square was a gorgeous mess—sprinkles everywhere, children sticky with victory, parents drunk on sugar and something softer. Sloane's booth was a battlefield of empty plates and happy ruin.

Graham helped break down, corners of his eyes warm with the kind of tired that feels like you've been useful. He stacked trays; she folded tablecloths. Their hands brushed and didn't have to apologize.

"Where to now?" he asked.

"Home," she said. "Shower. Nap. Then I come back for evening rush."

He nodded. "I'll meet you after. We'll clean. We'll celebrate. We'll eat tragic leftovers."

"Romance me with stale shortcake," she said. "How will I ever resist."

He tipped his head toward the gazebo where the kids had started an impromptu dance circle. "We'll start by embarrassing our children in public."

"Bold," she said. "I like it."

They crossed to the gazebo, ribbon fluttering from her apron string, and when the band stumbled into something approximating a slow dance, Graham held out a hand and said, "Front and center?"
"In every possible way," she said, and took it.

They swayed badly. Piper filmed. Miles groaned.

Someone yelled, "Get a room," and someone else yelled, "No, get a bakery," and Sloane laughed into Graham's shoulder until she felt the last of the bad week leave her body.

The sky mellowed to the color of peaches. The ribbon against her hip knocked gently like a friend asking to be let inside. The town went on around them—imperfect, opinionated, utterly theirs.

Sloane looked up at the man who had finally, publicly chosen to be seen with her and said, soft enough to be a secret and loud enough to be a vow, "Happy ending." He smiled against her temple. "Just the beginning."

CHAPTER THIRTEEN

The problem with kissing a man in front of the entire PTA is that the PTA does not forget.

By Monday morning, Sloane had:

- Three congratulatory texts
- Two passive-aggressive emails
- One anonymous Facebook comment that read: "Some people will do anything for attention."
- And a bouquet of strawberries dipped in chocolate left on the bakery counter with a note that said:

Front. Center. Always.
— G

She smiled at it like an idiot.

Then she panicked.

Because now it wasn't tension.

It wasn't flirting.

It wasn't "what if."

It was real.

And real meant vulnerable.

Graham showed up at 7:02 a.m. Not with coffee this time. With a toolbox.

"You said the mixer was rattling," he said, like this was a casual errand and not a deeply intimate domestic moment.

Sloane leaned against the counter. "So this is what we are now? Appliance maintenance partners?"

He didn't look up. "I prefer 'mutually invested adults.

She grinned. "That's way less sexy."

He looked at her then. Slowly. Deliberately.

"You don't need help making things sexy."

Her stomach flipped like a dramatic gymnast.

By mid-morning, the town had officially moved into Phase Two: Obsession.

Customers leaned in and whispered:

"So when's the wedding?"
"Are you moving in together?"
"Does this mean the cupcakes are named after him now?"

Sloane started charging $1 for every intrusive question.

By noon, she'd made $27.

Then came the moment.
The moment every small-town romance dreads.

Mindy walked in.

Alone. No

blazer.

No clipboard.

Just… a woman.

"Can we talk?" she asked.

Sloane blinked.
"Is this about the Detente Donuts?" she asked carefully.

Mindy exhaled. "No."

They sat at the front table — the one Sloane had imagined the first day she toured the bakery.

"Do you know what I was really afraid of?" Mindy asked.

Sloane folded her arms. "Enlighten me."

"That if you were allowed to be yourself… and people loved you anyway… then maybe I've been doing it wrong."

Oh.

Well.

That was not the villain monologue she'd prepared for.

Sloane softened despite herself.

"You're not doing it wrong," she said gently. "You're just… doing it tightly."

Mindy huffed a laugh.

"Is he good to you?" she asked.

Sloane didn't hesitate.

"Yes."

"Then I suppose I can tolerate the name."

"Which one?" Sloane asked.

"MILF."

They both smiled.

Truce. Not friendship.

But truce.

That night, Graham stayed late.

The kids were sprawled on the floor building a gingerbread town that looked like a crime scene.

Sloane wiped flour from her cheek and watched Graham laugh at something Miles said.

It hit her suddenly.

This wasn't dramatic.

This wasn't explosive.

This was steady.

And steady scared her more than fireworks ever had.

"You okay?" he asked quietly, noticing her watching.

She swallowed.

"This feels… safe."

He nodded.

"Good."

She stepped closer.

"I'm not used to safe."

He brushed his thumb along her jaw, slow and grounding.

"We'll practice."

And that felt like the most romantic thing anyone had ever said to her.

Chapter Fourteen
The Aftermath

Winning was supposed to feel good.

That's the part nobody tells you about small-town victory. The applause fades. The sugar crashes. The kiss goes viral.

And then the town decides what it thinks about it.

The bake-off had been loud and bright and glittered in all the right places. My strawberry shortcake sold out in under an hour. The kids screamed like we'd just won state. And Graham kissed me on stage in front of God, the PTA, and three separate Facebook Live streams.

It should've felt like triumph.

Instead, two days later, it felt like I'd lit a match and forgotten I was standing in a field of dry grass.

The first sign wasn't noise.

It was quiet.

Not between me and Graham. That part had softened. He'd been steady since the bake-off. Showing up without being asked. Fixing the back hinge on my storage door. Bringing Piper a book about constellations like he hadn't just detonated the social hierarchy of Willow Creek with one kiss.

No.

This was community quiet.

The bakery wasn't empty. But it wasn't warm either. Regulars still came in. Mrs. Delaney still ordered her cinnamon bourbon rolls. The high school girls still hovered near the display case pretending not to take selfies.

But people weren't just looking at the cupcakes anymore.

They were looking at me.

Whispers near the counter. Phones angled slightly too long in my direction. Conversations that dipped in volume when I approached.

I told myself I was being dramatic. I'd kissed the PTA president on stage. Of course people were staring.

Still.

It didn't feel like curiosity.
It felt like inventory.

By Wednesday, the internet did what the internet does best.

A post popped up in the Willow Creek Community Facebook group:

"Should school leadership be fraternizing with vendors who promote alcohol themes?"

Underneath it was a blurry photo of me and Graham mid-kiss.

I stared at it longer than I should have.

The angle was wrong.

Not from the front. Not from the crowd.

From the side of the stage.

Close.

Intentional.

I showed it to Graham that night at the counter.

"Who took this?" I asked.

He studied the image, jaw tight. "I don't know."

"You don't think that's weird?"

He hesitated just long enough to tell me he did.

That hesitation sat with me long after he left.

The next morning, I pulled up to the bakery and found my liquor distributor waiting outside. He shifted awkwardly when I unlocked the door.

"Morning," he said. "Got a call about your license."

My pulse did something unpleasant in my throat. "From who?"

"Didn't say. Just asked whether you were compliant."

"I am compliant."

"I know," he said quickly. "Just… figured I'd give you a heads up."

Heads up.

That phrase doesn't mean what people think it means.

It means something's coming.

Inside the bakery, the air felt thinner. Like the walls were listening.

By Thursday, there was a flyer taped neatly to my front window.

"Demand Accountability from Local Leadership."

Underneath, in smaller font: "Ask why your children's school is endorsing alcohol culture."

There was a QR code at the bottom.

Clean. Printed. Thought-out.

I didn't scan it.

I didn't need to.

I already knew what it would say. Words like inappropriate and unstable and think of the children.

I peeled it off slowly, aware of eyes on me from across the street. When I looked up, a woman pretended to check her phone. A car idled longer than necessary near the curb before pulling away too quickly.

I stood there for a second, telling myself I wasn't paranoid.

Small towns run on gossip.

But gossip doesn't usually come with printers and distribution strategies.

Inside, Piper was coloring at the counter.

"Mom," she said casually, "a lady at school asked if you were going to close."

My hands froze on the espresso machine.

"What lady?"

"I don't know. She said she heard you were in trouble."

The word trouble lodged somewhere behind my ribs.

"I'm not in trouble," I said, more firmly than necessary.

Piper nodded like that settled it. "I told her you're the boss."

I smiled.

But my jaw hurt from holding it there.

That night, after closing, Graham and I sat across from each other at the counter. The display case was empty. The lights were low. The room smelled faintly of sugar and citrus cleaner.

"This is coordinated," he said finally.

"Yeah," I replied. "It feels like someone pressed go."

He leaned forward. "Do you have any enemies?"

I almost laughed.

"Besides PTA moms with Pinterest boards?"

"I'm serious."

I tried to think of someone who would care enough to escalate like this. Someone with time. Someone with motive.

And then something flickered.

Antiseptic.

Fluorescent lights.

A clipboard.

A woman smiling just a little too tightly.
The image slipped away before I could grab it.

"You okay?" Graham asked.

"Yeah," I lied.

But something about this didn't feel like moral outrage.
It felt personal.

Friday morning, I got a voicemail from the health department requesting a "routine follow-up inspection."

I passed my last inspection easily. No violations. No warnings.

There was no reason for a follow-up.

Unless someone filed a complaint.

I stood alone in the quiet bakery, staring at rows of stainless steel and freshly scrubbed countertops.

I built this place with maxed-out credit cards and trembling hands. Painted the walls myself. Hung every light. Burned the first five batches of buttercream and tried again.

I am not ashamed of this place.

So why does it suddenly feel like I'm being audited for existing?

My phone buzzed again.

Unknown number.

I let it ring.

Then I texted Graham.

"I think this is bigger than gossip."

The typing bubble appeared almost immediately.

"I know."

And that's when something cold slid into my chest.

If this isn't random—

If this isn't just PTA politics—

Then someone has decided I need to go.

And that isn't about cupcakes.

I fully expected the harassment to continue…

But weirdly enough… nothing.

Yet.

CHAPTER FIFTEEN

125

Three weeks later, trying to forget about the events happening weeks prior, Sloane accidentally hosted a couples' bake night.

It started as a joke.

Then fifteen people signed up.
Then the local paper wrote an article titled:

FROM FROSTING TO FOREVER:

How Willow Creek's Booziest Bakery Became a Love Story

Sloane nearly died.

Graham framed it.

The first Couples' Night was chaos.

A man named Dennis cried over overworked dough.

Two women got competitive about piping techniques.

Someone burned caramel.

Sloane thrived.

Graham handled wine pours like a man born to supervise disaster.

At one point, Sloane caught him watching her again.

That look.

The one that said: I chose right.

She walked over, leaned in close, and whispered, "You staring?"

"Always," he said.

She kissed him quick — flour on her fingers, joy in her lungs.

Across the room, Piper fake-gagged dramatically.

"GET A ROOM," she yelled.

"We own one!" Sloane shot back.

The room erupted in laughter.

Later, when the guests left and the kids were asleep in a frosting coma in the office, Sloane and Graham stood alone in the quiet.

The bakery lights dimmed.

The square outside glowed softly.

He took her hand.

"I don't want to rush anything," he said. "But I don't want to pretend this is temporary either."

Her heart pounded.

"Okay," she said.

"Okay?" he asked.

"I'm not auditioning," she said. "And I'm not shrinking. If you're here, you're here with all of it."

He stepped closer.

"All of it."

She kissed him slow this time.

Not desperate.

Not frantic.

Intentional.
The kind of kiss that builds a life instead of chasing one.
When they pulled apart, she rested her forehead against his.

"You realize," she said softly, "this bakery started as survival."

"And now?" he asked.

She looked around at the mess. The laughter still echoing in the walls. The ribbon still hanging proudly. The life she'd built from spite and sugar.

"Now it's home."

He squeezed her hand.

"Good," he said. "Because I'm not going anywhere."

Outside, the lights of Willow Creek flickered gently.

Inside, flour dusted the floor like snowfall. And for the first time in a long time, Sloane wasn't bracing for the ending. She was looking forward to the next batch.

— CHAPTER SIXTEEN —

The Anonymous Tip

The first sign of trouble arrives at 9:13 a.m. in the form of a man wearing khaki pants and a badge that says COUNTY HEALTH INSPECTOR.

Sloane is mid-laugh with a customer—something about how "Detente Donuts" should come with a ceasefire agreement—when the man clears his throat like he's about to ruin her life politely.

"Ms. Matthews?" he asks.

Her stomach drops on instinct. Her body knows what doom feels like now. It comes in clipboards and neutral expressions.

"Yes," she says, wiping her hands on her apron. "If you're here about the 'Happy Ending' glaze, I can explain—"

"I'm here because we received an anonymous complaint," he says, already walking behind the counter like he owns the place.

Sloane's smile freezes.

"Anonymous," she repeats, voice calm, brain screaming.

The inspector nods. "Claims of improper labeling, possible alcohol being served to minors, and unsanitary practices."

Across the bakery, two customers turn their heads like prairie dogs smelling gossip.

Sloane's cheeks burn hot.

"Okay," she says, too bright. "That's insane."

The inspector begins opening drawers with the confidence of a man who has never been emotionally devastated by PTA moms.

She follows him, trying to keep her voice steady. "We have labeled adult-only items since day one. We have color-coded wristbands at events. We have a literal kids' menu called 'Behave-Yourself Berry Cups.' We are… aggressively compliant."

He checks her fridge temp.

He checks her storage.

He checks the sink.

Then he stops at the allergy binder—one of Graham's contributions—and flips through it slowly, eyebrows lifting.

"This is thorough," he says, like it pains him.

"Thank you," Sloane says, and doesn't let herself glance at the front window where she already knows half the town is watching.

The inspector turns to her. "Who handles your compliance?"

Sloane opens her mouth—

Graham appears at her shoulder like the answer to a prayer she didn't know she was allowed to pray.

"I do," he says. "Graham Walsh. Co-owner—" he catches himself, smooths it into something safer, "—co-operator in event compliance and safety procedures."

Sloane's heart flickers.

Co-owner?
He didn't say it like a joke.

The inspector looks between them. "Well. Mr. Walsh. It'll be you I speak to about the complaint documentation."

Sloane's jaw clenches so hard she's surprised her teeth don't crack. "Do we get to know who made the complaint?"

"No," the inspector says. "But I can tell you it was detailed. Someone knew what to say."

Sloane's eyes flick toward the window.

She doesn't see Mindy out there.

But she feels her anyway.

The inspector walks toward the front with a clipboard full of notes and a tone that says I don't care about your love story.
He stops at the door.

"For the record," he adds, "I didn't find enough to shut you down today. But I'll be back. This kind of complaint usually… escalates."

He leaves.

The bell jingles.

Silence drops like flour.

Sloane stands perfectly still, then turns to Graham.

Her voice comes out too quiet. "This is because of me."
Graham's face tightens. "No."

"It's because of the name. The vibe. The—" she gestures around, helpless, "—me of it all."

He steps closer. "It's because someone wants you to feel like you don't belong."

Sloane laughs once—bitter. "Congratulations. It worked."

His eyes sharpen. "Don't."

"Don't what?"

"Don't start shrinking now," he says, low. "Not when you've finally stopped apologizing."

Sloane's throat tightens. She wants to believe him. She does believe him.

But fear is louder than faith when you've been burned before.

"What if they shut me down?" she whispers. "What if I lose the bakery?"

Graham's hand finds her wrist—steady, grounding. "Then we fight."

"We?" she repeats.

He doesn't flinch. "We."

Her eyes sting.

Then Piper bursts from the back with a piping bag like a weapon. "Mom! The lady from the newspaper is outside!"

Sloane spins.

Outside, through the glass, she sees it. A reporter. Camera. Notepad.

And someone filming on a phone. Sloane's mouth goes dry.

Because this doesn't just feel like trouble anymore. It feels like a setup.

When Sloane opens the door, the reporter asks:

"Is it true you serve alcohol to children?"

Chapter Seventeen
Viral Frosting

It takes exactly twelve minutes for someone to make a TikTok titled:

"Willow Creek's MILF Bakery Serving Booze to Kids???"

It takes exactly one hour for it to hit the local Facebook groups.

It takes exactly two hours for the comment section to become a war zone.

And it takes exactly one look at the shaky video of Sloane saying, "Absolutely not—this is ridiculous," for her to realize:

The internet doesn't care what's true. It cares what's entertaining.

By 5 p.m., the bakery is half-full of supporters and half-full of people pretending they're customers while trying to catch her slipping.

Sloane is smiling so hard her face feels like it might crack.

Graham is in the corner making phone calls like a man who has decided he is done losing things.

"Principal Navarro is drafting a statement," Graham says, returning to the counter. "He's furious."

Sloane laughs without humor. "Cool. Will his fury pay my rent?"

Graham's jaw tightens.

"Sorry," she mutters. "That was… mean."

He looks at her. "It was scared."

Sloane swallows.

She doesn't even get time to breathe before her ex walks in.

And beside him?

New Girlfriend.

Again.

This time, she's not nervous.

She's smug.

She looks like she's wearing a decision.

Sloane's stomach sinks.

Her ex gives her the same fake concerned face he used to give her when she cried in the bathroom and he didn't want to deal with it.

"Hey," he says. "We saw the video."

Sloane blinks. "You don't live here."

"We still care," he says, like he deserves a medal.

New Girlfriend steps closer, eyes scanning the bakery like she's evaluating a property for purchase.

"We came to check on Piper," she says.

Sloane's blood turns to ice.

"Excuse me?"

The girlfriend tilts her head. "Just making sure she's safe."

Sloane's ears ring.

Graham takes one step forward. Not aggressive. Just present.

"Sloane's child is safe," he says calmly, but his voice has steel in it. "And this conversation isn't appropriate."

The ex exhales like the victim. "Look, we're not trying to cause drama. We're just… concerned about the environment."

Sloane laughs—sharp, dangerous. "The environment??
You mean the bakery? The one I built from nothing while
you were busy falling in love with 'less complicated'?"

A hush falls.

New Girlfriend's smile twitches. "You're emotional.
That's why people—"

"Oh, honey," Sloane cuts in, sweet as poison, "don't come
into my business and try to diagnose me. If you want
therapy, I can recommend someone."

The girlfriend flushes. "We're just thinking about Piper."

Graham's voice drops, lethal quiet. "Then leave."

The ex blinks. "Who the hell are you to—"

"I'm the man she comes home to," Graham says.

Sloane freezes.

So does the whole bakery.

The ex stares like he's been slapped by a Hallmark card.

New Girlfriend's mouth opens and closes.

Sloane's heart is trying to climb out of her throat.

Graham doesn't look at them. He looks at her.

And he says, softer, only for her: "If they're going to
come for you, they come through me first."

Her eyes burn.

But the moment doesn't get to stay sacred, because outside—
through the glass—Sloane sees flashing lights.

Not police.

Fire marshal.

Two of them.

Walking toward the door.

Sloane's stomach drops so hard she almost physically
sways
Because now it's not just a rumor.

It's an assault.

Chapter Eighteen
Smoke Alarm

Sloane doesn't remember moving, but suddenly she's behind the counter, heart pounding, hands shaking as she gestures toward the back hallway.

"It's not blocked," she says. "It's literally—"
The marshal holds up a hand. "We'll determine that."

He walks toward the back with the other marshal, and

Sloane follows like she's watching someone walk toward her open chest with a knife.

Graham stays close. Not touching. Just there.

The bakery feels like it's holding its breath.

The marshal checks the exit door. Checks the sign.
Checks the aisle width. Then stops.

And Sloane sees what he's seeing.

A stack of boxed supplies—new signage, seasonal décor, bulk napkins—set just slightly too close to the exit path.

Not enough that it's truly blocked.

But enough to make it look questionable.

Enough to make it arguable.

Sloane's knees go weak.

Graham's voice is calm. "We'll move it now."

The marshal nods, expression unreadable. "Do it."

Sloane reaches for the boxes with shaking hands.

She notices something as she lifts one.

It's heavier than it should be.

She opens it.

Inside, under the napkins, is a ziplock bag of mini liquor bottles.

Her vision tunnels.

"What… is that?" she whispers, like she's speaking from underwater.

Graham's eyes snap to it. His face drains.

The marshal's eyes narrow. "Those weren't disclosed on your inventory list."

Sloane's mouth goes dry. "Those aren't mine."

The marshal looks unimpressed.

Sloane's chest tightens. "I did not put those there."

The marshal looks at Graham. "Sir?"

Graham's jaw clenches.

"Sloane," he says quietly, "look at me."

She does.

His voice stays steady, but his eyes are blazing. "This is sabotage."

The marshal frowns. "Do you have proof?"

Sloane's mind races.

Then—like lightning—she remembers the camera Piper begged for. The one she set up after someone stole a tip jar two weeks ago.

The tiny security camera aimed at the back hallway.

Her throat tightens.

"I do," she says hoarsely.

She stumbles toward the office.

Pulls up the footage.

Fast forwards.

Her hands shake so hard she almost misses it.

But then she sees it.

A woman slipping into the back hallway during the lunch rush yesterday—hood up, ball cap low.

She moves quickly. Purposefully. Like she knows the layout.

She sets the box.

Adjusts it.

And then—right before she leaves—she glances up.

Straight into the camera.

It's not Mindy.

It's one of Mindy's PTA friends.

The one who laughed in the bathroom. The one who called Sloane unstable. Sloane's breath catches.
Graham leans closer, watching the footage, eyes hard.

The marshal stares at the screen, then back at Sloane.
"You should file a police report."

Sloane nods, numb.

Graham's hand finally lands on her back. Warm. Solid.
Keeping her upright.

But then the marshal adds:

"This doesn't change the fact your exit area isn't compliant today. You're closing early. You can reopen once you pass re-inspection."

Sloane's vision blurs.

Closing early. Re-inspection. Headlines. Rumors.

The bakery feels like it's slipping out from under her.

The marshals leave. The crowd disperses. The air goes thin.

Sloane stands in the wreckage of her dream and stares at the empty pastry case like it's a coffin.

Graham turns to her. "We're not letting them win."

Sloane laughs once, broken. "They already did."

"No," he says. "They hit you. That's not winning."

Sloane's throat tightens. "I can't do this again,

Graham. I can't rebuild my life every time

someone decides I'm too much."

His eyes soften. "Then don't rebuild alone."

She shakes her head. "You don't understand. If this becomes another thing I lose… I won't recover."

His voice drops, urgent. "Sloane. Look at me."

She does.

"I have lost before," he says quietly. "I know that terror. That helplessness. And I swear to you—" his voice cracks just slightly, "—I'm not letting you stand in it by yourself."

Sloane's breath catches.

Then her phone buzzes.

A notification.

A new post in the Willow Creek Moms Group.

Pinned.

From Mindy.

"For the safety of our children, please boycott MILF & Cookies until further notice."

Sloane's stomach drops.

Because the sabotage wasn't just behind her.

It was everywhere. And the worst part?

In the comments… were people agreeing.

Sloane whispers, devastated:

"They're going to ruin me."

And Graham says, deadly calm:
"Then we ruin them back."

Chapter Nineteen

Counter-Recipe

The bakery felt like a crime scene after the crowd left.

Not the dramatic kind with caution tape and flashing lights—just the quiet, humiliating kind where everything still smelled like sugar but the air tasted like loss.

Sloane stood behind the counter and stared at the phone in her hand like it had personally betrayed her. Mindy's post—pinned, bold, sanctimonious—glowed like a scar.

FOR THE SAFETY OF OUR CHILDREN… PLEASE BOYCOTT MILF & COOKIES UNTIL FURTHER NOTICE.

Below it, the comments multiplied like mold:

- "I knew something was off."
- "Why would she name it that if she wasn't inappropriate?"
- "My son said he saw wine bottles."
- "We should support family-friendly businesses."
- "Graham Walsh should be ashamed."

That last one punched harder than the rest, because it proved the point: this wasn't just about the bakery.

It was about punishing her for being visible.

Sloane swallowed, throat tight. "They're going to ruin me."

Graham stood at her side, shoulders squared like a man at the edge of a storm. He didn't look at the phone. He looked at her.

"Then we ruin them back," he said, voice calm in the dangerous way.

Sloane let out a broken laugh. "That's—Graham, that's not —"

"It is," he said. "But we're going to do it cleanly."

He reached past her and flipped the little sign on the door to CLOSED, then turned the deadbolt with a decisive click.

Sloane's heart thudded. The sound felt like a new chapter.

"I'm not built for public war," she said, voice thin. "I'm built for buttercream and bad decisions."

"You're built for surviving," he said. "And I'm built for structure. So we do what we do best."

He held up his phone. "First, we document. Then we respond. Then we expose."

Sloane blinked. "That sounds like a hostage negotiation."

"It is," Graham said. "They're holding your business hostage."

Sloane stared at him. "You're scary."

His mouth twitched. "I've been told."

She wanted to joke. She wanted to flirt. She wanted to make it lighter because heavy things were dangerous. But the bakery felt like it was holding its breath.

"What's the plan?" she whispered.

Graham exhaled like he'd been waiting for permission. "We're going to do three things tonight."

He lifted one finger. "One: you file a police report and provide the footage. Tomorrow morning."

Another finger. "Two: we get ahead of the narrative with the truth. Receipts. The compliance binder. The footage— at least the part that proves sabotage."

Another finger. "Three: we go to Navarro and demand the school issues a statement. The PTA does not get to run a smear campaign."

Sloane's mouth went dry. "And Mindy?"

Graham's eyes narrowed. "Mindy gets to explain why she pinned a boycott post without verifying facts."

Sloane's hands shook. She set her phone down and pressed her palms to the counter.

"I can't breathe," she admitted. "I feel like… this is just like my marriage. Like I'm screaming and everyone's already decided I'm the problem."

Graham didn't argue. He stepped closer until the space between them softened.

"I'm here," he said. "Look at me. Not them."

Sloane did. His eyes were steady. Real. Not judging.

"I'm scared," she whispered.

"I know," he said. "Be scared. We're doing it anyway."

Something in her chest loosened. Just a little.

Then the back door banged softly.

Piper's voice. "Mom?"

Sloane spun. Piper stood in the doorway in sparkly sneakers, clutching Sugarloaf's leash like a security detail.

Miles stood behind her, unusually quiet.

"Are we in trouble?" Piper asked.

Sloane's throat tightened. "No, baby."

Piper squinted. "Because people on my iPad said you're a 'bad influence.'"

Sloane froze.

Graham swore under his breath—quiet and lethal.

"Who said that?" Sloane asked, keeping her voice gentle.

Piper lifted the iPad. The Willow Creek Moms Group was open—someone had screenshotted Mindy's post and turned it into a meme. Sloane's neon sign was edited with devil horns.

Sloane's vision blurred.

Miles stepped forward, face pinched. "They were talking about my dad too."

Graham crouched to the kids' height, voice softening. "Listen to me. Your mom is not in trouble. Your dad is not in trouble. Adults say dumb things when they're scared and bored."

Piper frowned. "I'm bored."

Graham blinked. "Okay, well—this isn't fun bored." Piper considered that. "It kind of is."
Sloane let out a shaky laugh, then pulled Piper into her arms.

"We're okay," she whispered into her daughter's hair. "We're going to be okay."

Piper pulled back and looked at Sloane's eyes with terrifying accuracy. "Are you going to cry again in the dark bakery like last time?"

Sloane's breath caught.

Graham's gaze flicked to her—sharp, concerned.

Sloane swallowed. "Not tonight."

Piper nodded solemnly. "Good. Because I have a plan."

Sloane blinked. "You have a plan."

Piper's chin lifted. "Yes. We fight with glitter."

Graham sighed. "Please don't fight with glitter."

Piper ignored him. "Miss Mindy's friend—the one who smells like pickles and lies—she was here yesterday."

Sloane's blood chilled. "What?"

Piper nodded hard. "She came in and pretended to buy cookies and asked where the back door was. And she said, 'Kids shouldn't be around a place like this.'"

Graham's eyes sharpened. "Did she touch anything?"

Piper hesitated. "She went near the hallway." Sloane's stomach rolled.
Miles spoke quietly. "I saw her near the exit area. She was holding a box."

Sloane's heartbeat hammered. "You saw that?"

Miles nodded. "I didn't know it mattered."

Graham exhaled, slow. "It matters."

Sloane's hands clenched. She turned toward the office.

"That camera footage," she whispered. "We have her. We have proof."

Graham followed. "We do."

Sloane opened the footage again—rewound, zoomed.

And there she was: Mindy's friend—hood up, cap low, moving fast.

But this time, Sloane noticed something she hadn't before.

A lanyard.

A badge.

Not PTA.

Not school.

The badge flashed for one second when the hood shifted.

Sloane leaned closer until her breath fogged the screen.

Graham leaned over her shoulder, voice low. "That's… not a PTA badge."

Sloane whispered, "It says—"

Graham's jaw tightened. "County vendor access."

Sloane turned slowly. "How would she have that?"

Silence.

Then—Graham's phone buzzed.

A text from an unknown number:

STOP DIGGING.
WALK AWAY.
OR YOU'LL LOSE MORE THAN A BAKERY.

Sloane's blood turned to ice.

Graham's face didn't change, but the air around him did. Like he'd just shifted into a new mode.

He showed her the message.

Sloane stared. "That's… that's insane."

Graham typed with calm fingers.

WHO IS THIS?

Three dots appeared.

Then:

YOU DON'T WANT THIS.
LET IT GO.

Sloane's stomach flipped. "Graham…"

He looked at her. "We're not letting it go."

Sloane's voice shook. "What if it's—what if it's someone —"

"Then we get smarter," he said. "We don't get quiet."

He reached for her hand. "Pack up the kids. We're going to my sister's tonight. Somewhere safe, with cameras, and people around."

Sloane blinked. "Is this… like when you finally admit the monster is real?"

Graham's eyes didn't soften. "Yes."

Sloane swallowed. Then nodded. "Okay."

Piper popped her head into the office. "Are we doing the glitter war?"

Sloane managed a smile through fear. "Not yet, baby."

Piper narrowed her eyes. "That means yes later."

Graham muttered, "God help me."

And for a second, in the middle of dread, Sloane laughed.

Because even the scariest nights still had room for love.

Chapter Twenty
The Thread

The bakery didn't feel like hers anymore.

It felt like a set.

Like if she pushed too hard on one of the walls, it would tip over and reveal someone watching from the other side.

Sloane sat on the floor behind the counter at 1:13 a.m., legs crossed, back against the cabinets, laptop open, security footage paused mid-frame. The glow from the screen made the stainless steel appliances look clinical.

Interrogation lighting.

Graham sat across from her, knees bent, tie discarded somewhere hours ago. His sleeves were rolled up like this was a negotiation, not a bakery.

"Start at the beginning," he said quietly.

She scrubbed a hand over her face. "The beginning was Mindy being allergic to cleavage."

"No," he said gently. "The beginning of the escalation."

She stared at the footage again.

The woman in the hoodie.
The quick movement.
The lanyard flash.

Her stomach tightened.

"Okay," she whispered. "The fire marshal call."

Graham nodded once. "Pull the voicemail." She grabbed her phone and played it again. Routine follow-up inspection.

Normal tone.
No urgency.
But the timestamp made her frown.

"That was three days before the boycott post," she said slowly.

Graham leaned forward. "What?"

She replayed it. Inspection scheduled Tuesday morning. Mindy's post went live Friday afternoon.

Silence stretched between them.

"So someone flagged you before the public outrage," Graham said.

"Or someone planned to," she replied.

Her pulse ticked in her throat. She stood abruptly and went behind the counter, flipping open the compliance binder like she was proving something to the walls.

"All permits current. Liquor license updated. Vendor receipts clean."

She exhaled hard.

"This doesn't just happen. You don't get an inspection and a boycott and a planted bottle in the same week by accident."

Graham didn't argue.

He opened his laptop and logged into the PTA vendor portal.

"Walk me through the rearranged booth call," he said.

Sloane frowned. "They said I missed the final vendor meeting."

"And did you?"

"No."

She crossed the room, leaned over his shoulder.

The portal showed the vendor call log. Her name was listed. Attendance marked: Present. But the timestamp was wrong.

"That's not the time," she said.

Graham's fingers stilled.

"What time was it?"

"Five thirty," she said. "After closing. Piper was drawing unicorns on flour sacks."

He scrolled.

The attendance log showed 2:14 p.m.

Her stomach dropped. "I wasn't there at two fourteen," she whispered.

Graham's jaw tightened. "Who marks attendance?" he asked.

"The vendor coordinator."

"And that is?" Sloane swallowed.

"Mindy's friend. The pickle-scented one."

Graham closed the laptop slowly. The air felt heavier and they realized they weren't chasing smoke anymore.

They were touching fabric.

Thread.

By 2:03 a.m., the bakery floor was covered in printed screenshots.

Call logs.
Inspection emails.
Vendor shifts.
Facebook timestamps.

Sloane circled things with a pink highlighter like she was studying for a test she didn't sign up for.

"This doesn't align," she muttered.

Graham crouched beside her. "What doesn't?"

She tapped two sheets side by side. "The liquor distributor call warning me about a complaint."

Graham read it. "Thursday morning," he said.

She nodded.

"And Mindy's first public comment questioning alcohol was Friday afternoon."

Silence.

"So the complaint happened before the narrative," Graham finished.

"Yes."

She pressed her palms flat against the floor.

"This wasn't reaction. It was construction." Graham stared at the papers like he wanted to burn through them. "Okay," he said slowly. "What about the fire marshal?"

She shuffled through the printouts.

"Requested by—" she squinted at the header "—community concern submission."

"Anonymous?"

"Yes."

He leaned back against the cabinet and said, "That's vague enough to hide behind."

Sloane's heart pounded harder.

Her mind began to run.

Not frantic.
Focused.

"The booth relocation," she said suddenly.

Graham looked up.

"It wasn't about crowd control."

"No."

"It moved me closer to the service exit."

He went still.

"And that's where the bottles were planted," he finished.

She felt cold.

They stared at each other in the quiet bakery, flour dusted across the tile like ash.

At 2:47 a.m., Graham did something she hadn't expected.

He logged into the public school board funding database.

Sloane blinked. "What are you doing?"

"Seeing who signs vendor access approvals."

Her pulse ticked louder.

"That's… connected?"

"Maybe."

He scrolled through procurement approvals, maintenance access logs, event permits.

His jaw tightened.

"Vendor access badges are processed through the county office," he said. "But school events submit temporary clearance lists."

Sloane leaned closer.

"And?"

"And the request for expanded vendor access was submitted two weeks ago."
Her stomach flipped.

"Two weeks before the bake-off."

"Yes."

Silence.
Two weeks before anything public happened.

Before the whispering.

Before the booth relocation.
Before the boycott.

"Who submitted it?" she asked.

Graham's finger hovered over the screen.

"Redacted."

Her breath hitched.

"What do you mean redacted?"

"Administrative privacy marker."

"That's not normal."

"No," he agreed quietly. "It's not."

The clock above the espresso machine clicked to 3:11 a.m.

The bakery was still. But Sloane didn't feel alone anymore. She felt observed. She walked to the front window and looked out at the dark square of Willow Creek.

One streetlight flickered.

A car passed slowly.

Too slowly.
Her chest tightened.
She stepped back.

"This doesn't feel like PTA drama anymore," she said.

"It isn't," Graham replied.

She turned toward him.

"It feels like someone laid track."

Graham didn't answer immediately.

He stared at the spread of evidence on the floor.

Then he said, very carefully:

"Someone expected you to fail."

Her throat tightened.

"Or expected me to panic."

He looked at her then.

"You're not panicking."

She almost laughed.

"I'm sitting on the floor in flour pajamas building a
conspiracy corkboard in my own bakery."
His mouth twitched faintly.

"Strategically."

She swallowed.

"Whoever this is," she whispered, "they had access before
the outrage. They filed complaints before the posts. They
moved my booth before the bottles. They created a
narrative before the incident."
Graham nodded slowly.

"Yes."

She exhaled.

"And we're just now pulling the thread."

He stood.

Walked to the counter.

Picked up her phone.

"Then we pull it carefully."

Her stomach dipped.

"Careful how?"

He turned the phone toward her. An email notification sat unread.

From: County Vendor Office
Subject: Access Badge Usage Confirmation Required

Her pulse stuttered.

"I didn't apply for a badge," she whispered.
"I know," Graham said.

She stepped closer.

"What does it say?"

He didn't open it yet.

Instead, he met her eyes. "Whatever this is," he said quietly, "it started before the boycott."

Her breath went thin.

"And it's not random."

The espresso machine ticked as it cooled. The refrigerator hummed. The bakery held its breath.
Sloane felt it.

The shift. The moment you realize the storm wasn't spontaneous.

It was engineered.

Her phone buzzed in Graham's hand.

Unknown number. Again.

He didn't answer. Instead, he set the phone down slowly on the counter between them. And this time, neither of them looked away. Because whatever was coming next—

It wasn't gossip.

It was design.

And they had just found the thread.

Chapter Twenty-One

Lie Beneath the Sugar

Graham's sister's house smelled like laundry detergent and safety.

It was the kind of suburban calm that made Sloane want to sob—clean counters, soft lighting, a normal family dog who didn't wear frosting eyeballs. The kids settled instantly into a blanket fort like they were born for crisis slumber parties.

Piper named it "Operation Rescue Mommy."

Miles corrected her. "It's more like Operation Evidence."

Piper looked at him. "Nerd."

Miles blinked. "Correct."

Sloane sat at the kitchen table with Graham and his sister, Tessa, who had kind eyes and the hardened tone of a woman who'd dealt with Graham's emotional constipation for decades.

Tessa slid a mug of tea toward Sloane. "Drink. You look like you're vibrating."

Sloane laughed weakly. "I am."

Graham stood by the window, scanning the street like a man who wanted to control the entire world with his stare.

Tessa raised a brow at him. "Sit down before you start measuring the air quality."

Graham didn't move.

Sloane stared at the tea. "This is humiliating."

Tessa's voice softened. "Honey. Humiliation is when you trip in public and everyone laughs. This is harassment."

Sloane swallowed. "It feels like the whole town hates me."

Tessa leaned in. "The whole town doesn't. The loudest people do."

Graham finally sat, hands clasped too tight. "We need to move fast."

"Agreed," Tessa said. "What do we know?"

Sloane pulled out her phone, showed the footage, the lanyard, the threat text, the note in the window.

Tessa's expression changed—subtle, but real. "Okay. This is… more than PTA drama."

Graham nodded. "Someone has access beyond Mindy's friend group."

Sloane's throat tightened. "What if it's my ex?"

Graham's head snapped up. "Why would it be your ex?"

Sloane's stomach twisted. "Because this is the part where he makes sure I can't build anything without him resenting it."

Tessa exhaled. "That's not impossible."

Graham's jaw clenched. "He was in the bakery today."

Sloane nodded. "And his girlfriend was… weird. Not just smug. Like she came to poke a bruise."

Tessa tapped the table. "Okay. Here's what we do."

Graham blinked. "You have a plan."

Tessa's lips twitched. "I always have a plan. I'm your sister."

She lifted a finger. "One: police report first thing. Two: health department follow-up. Three: press statement with receipts. You control the story before the moms group does."

Sloane swallowed. "I don't want to be online. I want to bake."

Tessa nodded. "Then we make it one clean statement and we move on."

Graham's voice was low. "And Mindy."

Tessa looked at him. "Mindy is a symptom. Not the disease."

Sloane frowned. "She pinned the boycott."

"And she loves being the hero," Tessa said. "Which means she'll cling to whatever narrative makes her look righteous."

Sloane's eyes burned. "I hate her."

Graham's gaze flicked to her. "I know."

Tessa stood. "Give me your phone."

Sloane blinked. "What?"

Tessa held out her hand. "Your phone. I'm calling Mindy."

Graham's eyes widened. "You're calling—"

"Yes," Tessa said. "Because I have a gift. I can sound pleasant while eviscerating someone."

Sloane handed it over like she was giving away a weapon.

Tessa dialed and put it on speaker.

It rang once. Twice.

Mindy answered, breathless. "Hello?"

Tessa smiled—Sloane could hear it. "Hi, Mindy! This is Tessa Walsh. Graham's sister."

A pause. "Oh! Hi. Yes. Lovely."

"Just checking in," Tessa said brightly. "About your pinned boycott post."

Mindy's voice sharpened. "I stand by it. Parents have the right to—"

"Absolutely," Tessa cut in, still smiling. "And businesses have the right to sue for defamation."

Silence.

Sloane's heart hammered.

Mindy's voice dipped. "Excuse me?"

Tessa's tone stayed sweet. "You pinned a public post encouraging a boycott based on an unverified claim that children were served alcohol. That is not opinion. That is a damaging allegation."

Mindy swallowed audibly. "I... I didn't say—"

"You implied it," Tessa said. "And you platformed it. Which makes you liable."

Mindy's voice turned defensive. "People have been concerned for weeks. It's the branding, it's the—"

"Save it," Tessa said, and the smile dropped out of her voice. "Here's what's happening: you're going to unpin it, delete it, and post a correction by noon tomorrow. Or you're going to explain to a lawyer why you participated in a campaign to destroy a woman's livelihood."

Mindy's breath hitched. "That's dramatic."

Tessa chuckled. "No, Mindy. This is dramatic. A woman just found liquor bottles planted near her emergency exit. She has footage of someone doing it."

Silence.

Then Mindy's voice went smaller. "What?"

Tessa leaned over the phone like a blade. "You heard me."

Mindy hesitated. "Who... who would do that?"

Tessa's tone sharpened. "That's what I'm wondering. And since you're besties with the woman on camera, I suggest you start asking her questions. Fast."

Mindy's voice cracked a fraction. "I don't—she's not—"

Tessa cut her off. "Mindy. If you didn't organize this, prove it. You want to be the hero? Here's your chance."

A long pause.

Mindy spoke quietly. "Send me the footage."

Graham's eyes narrowed. "No."

Tessa ignored him. "We can send a screenshot of her face. If you can confirm who she is."
Mindy's voice sounded shaken. "I… I know who she is. That's —"

She stopped.

Sloane's stomach turned. "That's what?"

Mindy exhaled. "That's… complicated."

Tessa's voice went steel. "It's about to get uncomplicated. Unpin the post."

Mindy whispered, "Okay."

Tessa ended the call.

Silence filled the kitchen like smoke.

Sloane stared at Graham. "Your sister is terrifying."

Graham blinked. "I've told you."

Tessa handed Sloane her phone back. "Now," she said, "we wait and watch."

Sloane's hands shook. "What if she doesn't delete it?"

Tessa smiled. "Then we go nuclear."

Piper popped up from the blanket fort like a tiny mafia boss. "Is this the glitter war?"

Sloane laughed despite herself. "Not yet."

Piper nodded. "Okay. But I'm ready."

Miles said, dead serious, "I can hack the moms group."

Graham pinched the bridge of his nose. "Nobody is hacking anything."

Tessa sipped her tea. "Honestly, I'd let him."

Graham looked betrayed. "Tessa."

Tessa shrugged. "I'm pro-chaos when it's strategic."

Sloane's laugh cracked open into something real.
And then her phone buzzed.

A notification.

Mindy Clayborn edited a post.

Sloane clicked, breath held.

The pinned boycott post was gone.

In its place, a new post—less confident, less righteous:

"UPDATE: There is no evidence MILF & Cookies served alcohol to minors. I apologize for sharing unverified concerns. Please support local small businesses."

The comment section erupted.

Some moms apologized.

Some doubled down.

But the shift had begun.

Sloane stared at the screen, throat tight.

Graham's hand found hers under the table. "See?"

Sloane whispered, "It's not over."

"No," Graham agreed. "Because whoever planted that is still out there."

Tessa nodded. "And now they're going to panic."

Sloane's stomach dipped. "What does panic look like?"

Tessa's eyes narrowed. "Mistakes."

Sloane's phone buzzed again—this time, an email.

From the county vendor office.

Subject line: NOTICE OF INVESTIGATION – VENDOR ACCESS BADGE MISUSE

Sloane blinked. "Graham."

He leaned in and read. His jaw tightened.

"It says a badge was used under a stolen ID," Sloane whispered. "And they're contacting the badge holder."

Tessa's brows lifted. "Who is the badge holder?"

Sloane scrolled.

And went cold.

The name on the badge was not Mindy's friend.

It wasn't even a PTA mom.

It was—

Sloane Matthews.

Her breath vanished.

Graham's face drained. "That's impossible."

Sloane stared, shaking. "They're framing me."

A soft sound came from the doorway.

Piper, half-asleep, clutching Sugarloaf's leash like a teddy bear.

"Mom?" she whispered. "Are we in trouble again?"

Sloane swallowed hard, forcing her voice steady. "No, baby."

But her eyes filled anyway.

Because now it wasn't just gossip.

Now it was official.

Now it was a system.

And the scariest part?

Someone had the power to make her look guilty on paper.

Graham stood, slow and deliberate, like a man deciding what kind of monster he needed to become.

He looked at Sloane and said, low:

"Pack a bag. Tomorrow, we stop being polite."

Another text hits Graham's phone from the same unknown number:

WE CAN MAKE YOU DISAPPEAR, SLOANE.
ASK YOUR EX ABOUT THE BADGE.

And Sloane realizes—oh God—

This was never just about Mindy.

This was about someone who knew her past… and still wanted to control her future.

Chapter Twenty-Two
The Leak

By the time the badge email arrived, Sloane was too tired to cry.

The exhaustion had settled somewhere deeper than her bones — behind her eyes, under her skin, in the space where adrenaline had burned itself out and left something colder behind. The bakery lights were off, the chairs stacked, the square outside Willow Creek emptied into its usual polite darkness.

Graham had just left to grab coffee from the all-night gas station when her phone buzzed again.

At first, she didn't look.

She assumed it was another unknown number. Another warning. Another poorly spelled threat designed to feel bigger than it was.

But this time it was a notification.

Willow Creek Moms Group — New Post.

She shouldn't have opened it.

She knew that.
Still, she did.

The video was grainy. Cropped. Thirty-seven seconds long.

The caption read: "Interesting timing…"

Her breath slowed in a way that felt unnatural.

The footage was from her bakery. From the security camera. The angle wasn't wide — it had been zoomed and clipped, cutting out the hallway and most of the frame. What remained was a narrow view of the service exit and a figure moving near it.

Her.

Carrying a box.

The timestamp blinked in the corner. 8:42 p.m.

The night before the bottles were discovered.

The comments were already multiplying.

"Is that her?"
"That looks like the same exit area."
"Why was she near there after hours?"
"Does anyone else see what I see?"

Sloane stared at the screen, heart thudding, but not wildly. It was a contained thud. A steady awareness. The full footage — the one she and Graham had reviewed — showed far more. It showed her closing down the kitchen. It showed her checking the locks. It showed nothing suspicious. But this version didn't.

This version was surgical. It implied. It suggested. It planted doubt. She felt something unfamiliar then — not fear.

Calculation.

She replayed it twice more, forcing herself to watch without reacting. The crop line cut off the hallway. The crop line removed the moment she walked back into the kitchen. The crop line erased context.

This wasn't someone misunderstanding the footage. This was someone editing it.

Her phone buzzed again.

A direct message.

"Care to explain?"

She didn't answer.

Instead, she scrolled back to her own archived footage and pulled up the original file. The metadata confirmed what she already knew — the file had not been publicly shared.

She had it.

Graham had it.

Tessa had seen it briefly.
And she'd sent one screenshot — only one — to Mindy.
Her pulse ticked higher now. Not panic. Just narrowing.
Graham walked back in then, coffee in hand, shoulders
tight. He took one look at her face and stopped mid-step.
"What happened?"

She handed him the phone. He didn't speak while he
watched it. But something in his posture shifted. The calm
steadiness she'd come to rely on hardened into something
else. "They clipped it," he said evenly.

"Yes."

"Who has the original?"

She hesitated. "You do."

"Yes."

"Tessa saw it?"

"Yes."

"And Mindy?"

"She saw a still image. Not the file."

Graham set the coffee down carefully, like he didn't trust
his hands.

"This wasn't downloaded from your system," he said.
"This is screen capture."

Sloane's throat tightened. "So someone recorded it while
it was playing."

"Or accessed it directly."

The words settled between them.

Accessed.

She felt a thin line of cold move down her spine. The post continued climbing in engagement. Someone had already tagged the school board. Someone else had tagged the county vendor office. Her name was trending in a town with fewer stoplights than Starbucks. She sat down slowly behind the counter.

"I didn't send it," she said quietly.

Graham looked at her immediately. "I know you didn't."

She nodded, but the reassurance didn't land the way she wanted it to. Not because she doubted him — but because doubt had entered the room regardless.

"Who else would benefit from this?" she asked.

Graham exhaled slowly. "Someone who wants the narrative to shift from sabotage… to suspicion."

Sloane stared at the footage again. The box she was carrying was labeled.

Flour delivery.

Ordinary.

But in the cropped version, the label wasn't visible. Her body blocked it. It looked ambiguous. Deliberately ambiguous.

Her phone buzzed again.

This time it was a text from an unknown number.

"You should have stopped when we told you to."

Graham saw it over her shoulder. His jaw flexed.

"Block it."

She did. Another notification appeared almost immediately — this time from the school board office.

"Mandatory closed session meeting regarding conduct and liability. Mr. Walsh requested to attend."

Graham went still.

"They're calling you in," she said.

"Yes."

"About this."

"Yes."

The room felt smaller. She hated that she was thinking it. But she was. Who had access to the footage? Who had access to the vendor logs? Who had administrative redaction power? Who knew the inspection was scheduled before the boycott? She hated that the list included people sitting at her kitchen table two nights ago.

Graham met her eyes. "What are you thinking?"

She forced herself to answer honestly. "I'm thinking someone close enough to see the full picture… is only showing parts of it."

Silence.

Not accusatory.

Just heavy.

He didn't defend himself.

He didn't get angry.

He just nodded once, acknowledging the fear underneath it.

"That's fair," he said. The steadiness in his voice almost broke her.

"I don't want to turn into someone who doubts the only person standing next to me," she said quietly.

"You're not," he replied. "You're being careful."

He picked up his jacket. "They want me at the school board in an hour."

She stood. "Are they trying to remove you?"

"Maybe."

Her throat tightened: "Because of me."

He stepped closer.

"Because someone wants leverage."

She swallowed.

"Are you going to tell me everything they say?"

He didn't hesitate.

"Yes."

She believed him.

And yet, as the door closed behind him, she couldn't ignore the smallest fracture forming beneath the surface. Not between them. Around them. Trust wasn't gone.

But it was being tested.

And whoever was editing footage and planting evidence and sending threats understood one thing very clearly:

You don't destroy someone all at once.

You erode them.

Frame by frame.

Chapter Twenty-Three

Receipts and Reckonings

Graham drove like the road had offended him personally.

Sloane sat in the passenger seat with Piper's glitter backpack on her lap and the vendor email open on her phone, reading it over and over like the words would change if she stared hard enough.

NOTICE OF INVESTIGATION — VENDOR ACCESS BADGE MISUSE.
Badge Holder: SLOANE MATTHEWS.

Her stomach kept dropping in slow motion.

"How does my name end up on a badge?" she whispered, more to the universe than Graham.

Graham's jaw clenched. "It doesn't. Not legally. Not without a form. A copy of your ID. A signature."

Sloane's hands started to shake. "I didn't—"

"I know," he said quickly, softer. "I know you didn't."

It mattered that he didn't hesitate.

Her ex used to hesitate.
Her ex used to make "thinking" faces when she cried, like he was analyzing whether her feelings were convenient.

Graham just believed her. Immediately. Like it was the simplest thing in the world.

And somehow that made her want to sob harder.

Graham's phone buzzed again. He didn't look at it.

Sloane did, because apparently her nervous system hated peace.
Unknown number. Same as before.

LAST CHANCE.

STOP FIGHTING OR WE'LL MAKE IT WORSE.

Sloane stared. "Who is 'we'?"

Graham's voice was calm in a way that felt like ice. "Someone who thinks fear works on you."

Sloane let out a laugh that sounded broken. "It does."

Graham glanced at her. "Not forever."

He turned into a parking lot with the kind of sharp confidence that said the destination wasn't a suggestion.

Her ex's office. A glass building with a stupid minimalist sign and landscaping that looked paid to be boring.

Sloane's throat tightened. "Graham…"

"We're not texting him," Graham said. "We're not asking politely. He's either involved or he isn't, and we find out now."

Sloane's pulse hammered. "I don't want to see him."

Graham put the car in park and finally looked at her fully. "You don't have to be alone in that room again."

Sloane swallowed hard. "That sounds like a threat."

"It's a promise," he said.

Piper popped up from the back seat, chewing gum loudly, eyes bright with the chaos of a child who senses drama.

"Are we going to fight the man who hurt your feelings?" she asked.

Sloane blinked. "Piper."

Piper shrugged. "You cried in the laundry room that one time and said he was a 'thumb of a man.'"

Sloane choked. "I did not."

Graham's mouth twitched.

Piper leaned forward between the seats. "I'm ready. I have glitter."
Graham exhaled. "Please don't deploy glitter in a corporate office."

Piper nodded solemnly. "Okay. Pocket glitter only."

Sloane pressed her fingers to her temples. "This is my life."

Graham leaned in and kissed her forehead—quick, grounding. "This is our life."

Her heart did something stupid and tender.

They got out.

Graham took her hand like it was normal—like he wasn't leading her into the lion's den with the calm of a man who'd already decided who was leaving with power.

The receptionist smiled too brightly. "Can I help you?"

"Yes," Graham said politely. "We're here to see—"

Sloane's ex appeared from a hallway as if summoned by tension alone. He froze when he saw her. Then his eyes flicked to Graham's hand on hers and narrowed.

"Sloane," he said, like her name still belonged to him. "What—"

"Save it," Sloane said, voice shaking but present. "I got an email. My name is attached to a vendor badge. Someone texted Graham to ask you about it."

The ex's face changed fast. Too fast.

A blink.
A tight jaw.
A calculated inhale.

Graham saw it too. His posture shifted slightly.

"What did you do?" Graham asked, quiet.

The ex scoffed, performing confusion. "I have no idea what you're talking about."

Sloane's chest tightened. "Don't do that. Don't make me feel crazy. Not again."

The ex's eyes flicked to the receptionist, then to Piper— who was standing behind Sloane with the intensity of a tiny bodyguard.
He forced a smile. "Let's talk privately."

Graham didn't move. "No."

The ex blinked. "Excuse me?"

Graham's voice was calm and precise. "No private rooms. No closed doors. No intimidation. We talk here."

Sloane's ex's nostrils flared. "This is my workplace."

"And that's her identity on a badge," Graham said. "So choose wisely."

A silence landed.

Sloane's ex leaned closer to Sloane, dropping his voice. "You think I'd risk my job to mess with your… bakery drama?"

Sloane's throat went hot. "I think you've risked worse to punish me for leaving."

He laughed once, sharp. "You're being dramatic."

Graham's eyes narrowed. "Answer the question."

The ex's smile slipped. "Fine. I know a guy at the county vendor office. I asked a favor once. That's it."

Sloane went cold. "You asked a favor."

"I asked to get an expedited badge for an event," he snapped. "For a client. Weeks ago."

Sloane stared. "A badge… in my name."

His eyes flickered.

Graham's voice turned lethal quiet. "Why would you use her name?"

The ex's throat worked. "I didn't. I—" he stopped, then tried again, "I gave them a contact. A name. I didn't think it mattered."

Sloane's vision tunneled. "You used my name as a throwaway."

He rolled his eyes like she was exhausting. "It's not like I thought it would—"

"It did," Sloane said, voice shaking. "It did."

Piper suddenly stepped forward, tiny chin lifted. "You're a thumb," she said clearly.

The receptionist choked.

Sloane almost laughed—almost cried.

Her ex's face flushed. "Who the hell—"

"I'm her daughter," Piper said. "And my mom is brave and you're a liar."

Graham didn't even flinch. He looked at the ex like he was a file to be closed.

"Give us the name," Graham said. "The county contact."

The ex hesitated.

Graham took out his phone and held it up. "Then I call an attorney and a detective and you explain why you knowingly misused her identity for a county badge."

The ex's mouth opened. Closed. He looked around like he wanted support from the air.

Then he muttered a name.

"Brent," he said. "Brent Halvorsen."

Graham's eyes sharpened. "Title?"

"Vendor coordinator. Contracted."

Sloane's stomach flipped. "Contracted with who?"

The ex swallowed. "Third party."

Sloane stared. "So not even county staff."

Her ex shrugged. "It was easy."

Easy.

That word made her want to scream.

Graham stepped closer, voice like steel wrapped in velvet. "You're going to text Brent right now. In front of us. And you're going to ask him why your 'favor' turned into harassment of Sloane."

The ex scoffed. "He won't answer."

"Text him," Graham repeated.

The ex hesitated—then did it. His thumbs moved fast, annoyed.

Sloane watched his phone like it was a snake.

Three dots appeared immediately.

Then a message popped up.

Brent:
Stop. Not here. Call me.

Sloane's heart slammed.

Graham's gaze locked on the ex. "Not here," he echoed. "Interesting."

Sloane's voice came out as a whisper. "He's scared."

Graham nodded once. "Good. Fear makes people sloppy."

The ex shoved his phone in his pocket. "Look, I didn't—
this isn't—"

Sloane stepped closer, eyes blazing. "You used my name
like it was nothing. You handed someone the weapon and
acted surprised when they aimed it at me."

Her ex's face hardened. "You're always the victim."

Sloane's jaw clenched. Then—calm, sharp, final:

"No. I'm the survivor."

She turned away from him.

And Graham—Graham didn't even look at the ex again.
He just took Sloane's hand and guided her toward the
door as if he'd done this a thousand times: exit toxic
rooms, protect what matters, don't negotiate with people
who mistake your kindness for weakness.

Outside, Sloane sucked in air like it was the first time
she'd breathed in months.

Piper hopped beside her. "Did we win?"

Sloane stared at the sky. "We got the name."

Graham's phone buzzed.

Unknown number again.

YOU'RE MAKING THIS WORSE.
THE TOWN WILL TURN.
WATCH.

Sloane's stomach sank. "What does that mean?"

Graham's eyes went distant.

Then his phone rang.

A number saved as NAVARRO.

Graham answered. "Navarro."

Navarro's voice sounded tight. "Graham… you need to get to the school. Now."

Graham's face drained. "Why?"

Navarro swallowed audibly. "Because someone filed a report with CPS."

Sloane's blood went ice-cold.

Navarro continued, voice low: "They're alleging alcohol exposure in the home."

Sloane's ears rang.

Graham's voice turned deadly quiet. "Sloane didn't—"

"I know," Navarro said. "But it's filed. It's in motion. You need to move fast."

Sloane's knees went weak.

Piper looked up at her. "Mom?"

Sloane swallowed hard, trying to keep her voice steady. "We're okay, baby."

But her hands shook.

Because the fight had just changed.

It wasn't about the bakery anymore.

It was about her motherhood.

And that was the one thing she would burn the entire town down to protect.

As they rush to the car, Sloane gets a Facebook notification:

A new anonymous post in the Moms Group—
a photo of Piper at the bake-off holding a sample cup—
captioned:

"This child should not be in that environment."

That night, Piper crawled into my bed without asking.

She didn't cry. She didn't ask questions. She just laid there quietly, staring at the ceiling.

"You think I don't notice," she said finally.

"Notice what?" I asked.

"When you're pretending."

My throat tightened.

She turned her head toward me, eyes too old for seven.

"You pretend you're not scared so I won't be scared. But I'm not scared of bad people. I'm scared of you being sad."

That one hurt. I brushed her hair back slowly. "I'm not sad," I whispered.

"You are," she said gently. "But you're also strong. And strong people can be sad."

I swallowed hard and then asked"Do you wish you had a different mom?" I asked before I could stop myself.

She frowned like the question offended her. "No. I wish other people had better ones." Then she tucked herself against me and fell asleep like the world hadn't just tried to tilt sideways.

And I realized something terrifying and holy at the same time:

I wasn't just fighting for a bakery.

I was fighting for the version of bravery she was learning from me.

Chapter Twenty-Four
No More Nice
In Place

They didn't go home.

They went straight to the school.

Sloane sat in the principal's office with Piper's small hand clenched in hers and Graham's presence pressed against her side like a shield. Piper swung her legs under the chair, blissfully unaware of how the world could weaponize a rumor.

Navarro sat behind his desk with his jaw tight and a folder open. Tessa had arrived ten minutes earlier—hair pulled into a bun that screamed "I will litigate you in public."

Sloane had never been so grateful for another woman's fury.

Navarro spoke carefully. "CPS reports are confidential. I can't tell you who filed. But I can tell you what it alleges."

Sloane's mouth went dry. "Say it."

Navarro glanced down. "That your child is being exposed to alcohol, adult content, and neglect due to your business environment."

Sloane's vision blurred.

Tessa's voice was razor-sharp. "Adult content."

Navarro nodded grimly. "They referenced the name of the bakery, and the 'Happy Ending' item. They attached screenshots of the Moms Group posts and the viral TikTok."

Sloane's throat tightened. "So the internet is… evidence now."

Graham's voice was low. "They're building a paper trail."

Navarro looked apologetic. "CPS will have to follow up. That doesn't mean they'll find anything. But it's stressful, and I—" he exhaled, "—I'm sorry."

Sloane stared at the desk until her eyes stopped stinging. She forced a breath in. Another.

"Okay," she whispered. "Then we give them nothing to find."

Graham squeezed her hand. "We will."

Piper suddenly said, "Is this about Miss Mindy?"

Everyone froze.

Sloane blinked. "Piper—"

Piper shrugged. "She doesn't like us. She always looks at you like you stepped on her shoes."

Tessa muttered, "Accurate."

Navarro's eyes flicked to Graham. "I'm going to be blunt," he said. "This is coordinated."

Graham nodded. "Yes."

Navarro leaned back, voice lower. "The board chair is pressuring me to 'distance the school' from MILF & Cookies."

Sloane's stomach dropped. "The board chair?"

Navarro hesitated, then said it: "Mindy's husband."

Sloane went still.

Of course. Of course. Of course.

It wasn't just PTA moms being petty.

It was power.

It was a family with influence and community control and the ability to make Sloane's life miserable with a single phone call.

Graham's voice was ice. "We're dealing with the Clayborns."

Tessa nodded. "Bingo."

Sloane's heart hammered. "Okay," she said again, but this time it didn't sound small. It sounded like a match striking.

She lifted her chin. "Then we stop playing defense."

Graham's brows lifted slightly. "Sloane…"

She looked at him. "Front and center, right?"

His gaze held hers, steady. "Right."

Sloane stood.

Navarro blinked. "What are you doing?"

Sloane's voice came out calm, clear, terrifyingly controlled. "I'm going to tell the truth."

Tessa's eyes glittered. "Yes you are."

Graham frowned. "Where?"

Sloane reached into her bag and pulled out her phone. Opened the camera. Turned it toward herself.

Graham's eyes widened. "Sloane—"

She didn't look away. "If they're going to make a story, I'm going to own the narrative."

Tessa nodded. "Keep it factual."

Sloane inhaled. Hit record.

Her voice was steady, but her eyes were bright with the truth.

"Hi," she said into the camera. "This is Sloane Matthews, owner of MILF & Cookies in Willow Creek."

She swallowed hard, and pushed through.

"I want to address rumors circulating online. We do not—ever—serve alcohol to minors. We follow strict labeling and compliance procedures, including allergy and ingredient documentation. This week, our bakery received multiple anonymous complaints."

She paused, then continued.

"Today we discovered evidence of sabotage. We have security footage of an individual planting items near our emergency exit—items that do not belong to our business. We are filing a police report, cooperating with county investigations, and we will not be bullied into silence." She looked straight into the camera.

"And if you've posted, shared, or encouraged a boycott based on unverified claims, I ask you to correct it. Not for me—for integrity. For truth."
Her voice shook slightly, but her spine didn't.

"And lastly," she added, softer, "I am a mom. My

daughter is safe, loved, and cared for. If anyone is using my child as a pawn in this… you should be ashamed of yourself."

She ended the recording.

Silence.

Even Navarro looked stunned.

Graham stared at her like she'd just set the town on fire with a single match.

Tessa exhaled. "That was… excellent."

Sloane's hands shook. "Post it."

Graham's voice was low. "If you post it, the war escalates."

Sloane looked at him. "It already escalated when they brought CPS into it."

Graham didn't argue.

He nodded once. "Okay. We post."

Tessa leaned in. "We post on your bakery page, your personal page, and we tag the county health department statement once we have it. Also—" her smile turned dangerous, "—we request a public retraction from Mindy."

Sloane's mouth tightened. "She'll refuse."

Tessa shrugged. "Then she'll look guilty."

Navarro stood. "I'll issue a statement from the school about the fundraiser compliance procedures. And I'll include that your kids' cups were alcohol-free."

Sloane's eyes filled. "Thank you."

Navarro nodded. "I hate bullies."

Graham's phone buzzed again.

Unknown number.

POST IT AND WE POST OURS.

Sloane's heart slammed. "They have something."

Graham's face went hard. "Or they're bluffing."

Sloane's mind flashed—her divorce. Her ex. The way shame spreads when someone controls the narrative.

She whispered, "What if they have something from my past? Something I said… something I did when I was broken—"

Graham stepped close. "Then we face it. Together."

Sloane stared at him. "You don't know everything."

Graham's eyes softened. "I don't need to. I just need to know who you are now."

Her breath caught.

Tessa interrupted, practical. "Post the video. Now."

Sloane nodded.

They posted.

Within minutes, it spread like wildfire.

Support poured in.

People shared their own stories about rumors and small-town cruelty.

A few of the mean moms doubled down, but the tide shifted—because Sloane wasn't hiding anymore. She was standing in the light.

Then…

A new post appeared.

From an anonymous account.

A screenshot of Sloane's old divorce filings.

Highlighted lines. Out of context.

A caption:

"SHE'S UNSTABLE. READ THE DOCUMENTS."

Sloane went cold.

Her hands shook. Her throat tightened.

Navarro stared. "That's… confidential."

Tessa's eyes narrowed. "Not if someone has access."

Graham's jaw clenched so hard it looked painful.

Sloane whispered, "My ex."

Graham's eyes snapped to hers. "Or someone who knows him."

Tessa was already moving. "We're done guessing."

She grabbed her keys. "We go to Mindy's."

Sloane blinked. "What?"

Tessa's smile was all teeth. "You want suspense? Here it is. We confront the source at the top. In person."

Graham's voice dropped. "Tessa…"

"No," Tessa said. "They went after a child. We are not sending polite emails."

Sloane's pulse hammered. Fear and adrenaline and rage braided into something powerful.

She stood.

"Okay," she said, voice steady. "Let's go."

Piper looked up. "Are we doing glitter war now?"

Sloane crouched to her level, brushing her hair back. "Not glitter, baby."

Piper frowned. "Then what?"

Sloane smiled—soft but fierce. "Truth."

Piper nodded solemnly. "Truth war."

Miles added quietly, "I'll bring evidence."

Graham rubbed his face, caught between

horror and admiration. "This is my life."

Tessa clapped once. "Welcome."

They walked out of the school like a storm front—Sloane holding her daughter's hand, Graham at her shoulder, Tessa leading like she'd been waiting for this moment her whole life.

And as they climbed into the car, Graham's phone buzzed one more time.

Unknown number.

DON'T COME TO THE CLAYBORNS' HOUSE.
YOU WON'T LIKE WHAT YOU FIND.

Sloane stared at the screen.

Then looked at Graham.

"I'm going anyway," she said.

Graham's voice was low and sure. "Me too."

The Clayborn house comes into view— perfect lawn,
bright porch lights.

And on the front step…
is a familiar figure in heels.

New Girlfriend.

Waiting.

Smiling.

Like she's been expecting them.

Chapter Twenty-Five

The Porch Light

The Clayborns' house looked like the kind of place where nothing bad was allowed to happen.

Perfect hedges. White columns. A wreath on the door in April like seasonal joy was a requirement. The porch light cast a flattering glow across a front step that had never known a package thief or a broken promise.

And standing in it—heels planted, hair glossy, smile calm —was New Girlfriend.

Sloane's stomach went tight and cold. She wasn't sure if she wanted to scream or laugh.

Tessa parked in the driveway like she owned the deed.

Graham's hand hovered near Sloane's knee, not touching, but there. A question. Permission. Support.

Sloane inhaled and said softly, "Remember—front and center."

Graham nodded. "Always."

Piper leaned forward from the back seat. "Is that the lady who smells like perfume and lies?"

Sloane bit the inside of her cheek. "Lower your voice."

Piper whispered louder. "Sorry. Perfume and betrayal."

Miles murmured, "This seems like a confrontation scene."

Tessa opened the door. "It is."

They stepped out together.

New Girlfriend's smile widened as they approached, but her eyes flicked quickly—measuring each person, counting allies, clocking the kids like they were leverage.

"Hi, Sloane," she said brightly. "Hi, Graham."

Graham's tone was flat. "Why are you here?"

New Girlfriend lifted her brows. "I could ask you the same."
Sloane stopped at the bottom step. "Move."

New Girlfriend didn't. She held out her hands like she was a mediator at a hostage exchange. "I don't think you should go in there."

Tessa laughed once—short and sharp. "That's adorable. Step aside."

New Girlfriend's gaze flicked to Tessa. "You must be the sister."

Tessa tilted her head. "You must be the problem."

New Girlfriend exhaled, like they were exhausting. "Mindy is inside. She's... not doing well."

Sloane's lips parted. "Oh, is she? That's tragic. I should send her a 'Get Well Soon' cupcake shaped like accountability."

New Girlfriend's smile twitched. "Sloane, please. This is bigger than the PTA. Bigger than gossip."

Graham's eyes narrowed. "Then say what you came to say."

New Girlfriend hesitated. For a fraction of a second, her mask slipped—fear, or guilt, or something close.

Then she said, quietly, "Your ex is involved."

Sloane's body went still.

The air snapped.

Piper's hand tightened on Sloane's fingers.

Graham's voice dropped. "How."

New Girlfriend swallowed. "The badge. The posts. The screenshots. He's been feeding someone information."

Tessa's eyes sharpened. "Someone like... Mindy's husband?"

New Girlfriend didn't answer directly. Instead she glanced toward the door—toward the warm, perfect house.

"He's inside," she said softly. "Mr. Clayborn."
Sloane's heart pounded. "Mindy's husband."

New Girlfriend nodded once. "He's the one with the connections. He's the one who's been… escalating."

Sloane stared at her. "And you're telling me because… what? You grew a conscience?"

New Girlfriend's face tightened. "Because I'm tired."

"Tired?" Sloane repeated, incredulous. "Of what? Being part of a smear campaign?"

New Girlfriend's eyes flashed. "Of being used."

Graham's gaze went hard. "Used by who."

New Girlfriend exhaled. "By your ex. By Clayborn. By all of it."

Sloane's brain tried to catch up. "Why would you be used? You're… you."

"Exactly," New Girlfriend said quietly. "I'm convenient. I'm 'stable.' I'm 'presentable.' I'm the kind of woman men use to prove a point."

Sloane's throat tightened on an old, familiar pain—one she didn't want to share with this woman, but recognized anyway.

Tessa crossed her arms. "So you're the messenger."

New Girlfriend nodded. "And the evidence."

Graham blinked. "What evidence."

New Girlfriend reached into her purse and pulled out her phone. Her hand shook slightly.

"I have texts," she said. "From your ex. From Clayborn."

Sloane's chest compressed. "Show me."

New Girlfriend swiped, then held out her phone.

Sloane read.

Her vision tunneled.

Because there it was—her ex's words, casual and cruel:

EX: She can't keep getting away with playing the victim.
EX: She needs to learn she's not special.
EX: You said Clayborn can pressure Navarro? Good.
EX: The bakery name alone should get her buried.

Sloane's stomach rolled.

She scrolled again. Another thread. Clayborn's number.
His tone clinical:

CLAYBORN: Keep it to "child safety." Optics matter.
CLAYBORN: Make sure it looks organic.
CLAYBORN: Use the badge angle. County won't want
scandal.

Sloane's hands shook so hard she nearly dropped the
phone.

Graham leaned in, reading. His face didn't change much
—but the air around him did. Like a door closing.

Tessa whispered, "Oh, we've got him."

Sloane swallowed hard. "Why would Mindy allow this?"

New Girlfriend's mouth tightened. "She didn't start it. But
she didn't stop it either."

Sloane stared at the porch. "So she's not the mastermind."

New Girlfriend's eyes slid toward the door again. "No."

Then she added, quieter, "She's the cover."

Sloane felt rage bloom—hot, clean, clarifying.

She handed the phone back slowly. "Okay."

Graham's voice was low. "Okay?"

Sloane looked at him. "We go in."

New Girlfriend's eyes widened. "Sloane, you don't understand—Clayborn is… charming. He'll spin it. He'll deny it. He'll—"

Tessa cut in. "We're not here to debate. We're here to expose."

Sloane nodded. "And reclaim."

New Girlfriend stepped aside finally.

Tessa climbed the steps first like she was storming a castle. Graham followed, then Sloane with Piper's hand in hers and Miles close behind.

Sloane knocked once.

The door opened almost immediately.

Mindy stood there in a silk robe that screamed "I'm the victim," eyes red, mascara smudged like she'd practiced it in the mirror. For one second, she looked genuinely startled.

Then her gaze landed on Sloane, and something defensive snapped into place.

"Sloane," Mindy breathed. "You can't be here."

Sloane smiled politely. "I'm sorry. Did I interrupt your campaign meeting?"

Mindy's face went pale. "What are you talking about?"

Tessa stepped forward. "We're talking about defamation, harassment, and misuse of county access badges."

Mindy's mouth opened. Closed. She glanced behind her, and Sloane saw it:

A man in a collared shirt standing in the foyer—Mr. Clayborn—with the calm expression of someone who had never been told "no" in his entire life.

He smiled at Graham first, like they were equals. "Graham. This is… unexpected."

Graham's voice was arctic. "It shouldn't be."

Clayborn's smile didn't move. "Come in."

Sloane stepped forward without waiting for permission. "No thanks. We'll keep it public."

Clayborn's eyes flicked to the street, then back to her. "Sloane, isn't it? I've heard a lot."

Sloane's smile sharpened. "I'm sure you have."

Clayborn clasped his hands. "This is all very dramatic. I'm sure there's been misunderstandings."

Tessa laughed. "We have texts."

Clayborn's expression didn't flicker. "Do you."

Graham spoke finally, voice controlled but lethal. "We do."

Clayborn's gaze slid to New Girlfriend at the edge of the porch. "Ah."

For the first time, the man's composure cracked—just a hairline fracture. Enough for Sloane to see it.

Enough to know: This hit a nerve.

Clayborn's tone stayed smooth. "Whatever you think you know, I suggest you take a breath and consider—"

Sloane cut him off. "Consider what? That you're powerful? That you can whisper 'child safety' and make my daughter's life collateral damage?"

Clayborn's jaw tightened. "I'm concerned about the community."

Sloane's voice shook, but she didn't back down. "You're concerned about control."

Piper tugged Sloane's hand and whispered, "Mom, he has mean eyes."

Sloane squeezed her hand. "I know, baby."

Clayborn noticed Piper then. His smile turned performative. "Hello there."

Piper stared him down. "Don't talk to me."

Mindy gasped. "Piper!"

Piper shrugged. "You told everyone my mom is bad. That's mean. I don't like you."

Mindy's face crumpled. "I didn't—"
"Yes, you did," Piper said simply. "On Facebook."

Silence slammed down.

Clayborn exhaled slowly. "Let's not involve children."

Sloane's laugh was cold. "You already did."

Tessa stepped in. "Here's what's going to happen. You're going to issue a correction, publicly. Your wife is going to retract the post and apologize. You're going to cease contact with any county contractor about Sloane's business. And if you don't?"

Clayborn's eyes narrowed. "And if I don't?"

Graham took one step forward. "Then I take it to the county. The press. The school board. The state licensing office. And I don't stop."

Clayborn stared at him. "You're threatening me."

Graham's voice didn't rise. "I'm promising you."

Mindy's breathing turned shallow. "Graham—please—"

Sloane looked at Mindy. Really looked.

"Did you know?" she asked quietly.

Mindy's eyes filled. "I—"

Sloane's voice sharpened. "Did. You. Know."

Mindy's shoulders sagged. "I knew he was… trying to protect the PTA."

Sloane's throat tightened. "Protect it from what? A bakery with a neon sign?"

Mindy whispered, "From embarrassment."

Sloane nodded slowly. "So you chose to embarrass me instead."

Mindy's face crumpled.

Clayborn stepped forward, a hand hovering toward Mindy's shoulder—possessive, controlling. "This is enough."

Sloane's pulse pounded. She looked him dead in the eye.

"No," she said. "This is the beginning." She turned to New Girlfriend. "Send me the screenshots." New Girlfriend nodded, face pale.

Clayborn's smile returned—thin. "You think screenshots will beat influence?"

Sloane smiled back—warmer, more dangerous. "No."

Then she lifted her phone, clicked record, and aimed it at Clayborn's face.

"But the truth will."

Clayborn's expression finally changed.

"Turn that off," he said, voice tight.

Sloane's smile didn't move. "No."

Graham's hand slid to the small of her back—steady, anchoring.

Sloane spoke clearly into the camera. "Hi. This is Sloane Matthews. I'm standing on the porch of Mr. and Mrs. Clayborn—leaders in our community—because my business and my child have been targeted."

Clayborn's jaw clenched.

Sloane continued. "We have evidence of sabotage, harassment, and misuse of county vendor credentials. We have messages implicating individuals connected to leadership in the PTA and school board."

Clayborn stepped forward. "Stop."

Sloane didn't. "If anything happens to me, my child, or my business after this—everyone will know exactly where to look."

She ended the recording.

The porch went dead quiet.

Clayborn stared at her like she'd become something he couldn't buy or bully.

Then he said softly, dangerously, "You're making a mistake."

Sloane's voice was calm. "No."

She took Piper's hand. Looked at Graham.

"I'm making a choice."

They walked back down the steps.

New Girlfriend moved with them. Tessa followed last.

And as they reached the driveway, Sloane's phone buzzed with a new notification.

New email: COUNTY VENDOR OFFICE — REQUEST FOR MEETING (URGENT).

Graham's phone buzzed too.

Unknown number. Final message:

YOU JUST DECLARED WAR.

Sloane swallowed.

Then looked at Graham.

"Good," she whispered.

As they drive away, a car pulls out behind them— headlights off, following.

Chapter Twenty-Six

The Bake Sale DISASTER

They lost the tail three turns later.

Not because the tail gave up—because Tessa, in her terrifying competence, took three unnecessary roundabouts like she was escaping a spy movie.

"Are we being chased?" Piper asked, delighted.

"No," Sloane said quickly.

Miles leaned forward, dead serious. "Yes."

Graham said nothing—just stared out the windshield like he was cataloging the shape of every threat.

When they reached Tessa's house again, Graham parked in the garage and shut the door behind them like the world outside was no longer allowed in.

Sloane's hands were shaking. "That was… insane."

Tessa nodded. "Yes."

New Girlfriend stood near the kitchen island like she didn't know what to do with herself now that she'd chosen a side.

Graham finally looked at her. "Why did you help."

New Girlfriend's throat worked. "Because he—" she swallowed, "—your ex told me I was different. That I was 'safe.'"

Sloane's chest tightened.

New Girlfriend's voice cracked. "Then I saw what he did to you and realized… 'safe' was just his word for controllable."

Sloane didn't soften all the way, but something in her loosened. "You knew he was feeding Clayborn?"

New Girlfriend nodded. "He bragged about it. Like it was clever. Like it was justice." Her eyes filled. "I didn't know it would become… this."
Tessa's tone was blunt. "Men who want to punish women always start small. Then they get bold."

Graham's jaw clenched. "Send the screenshots. Every one."

New Girlfriend nodded and started forwarding texts, threads, timestamps—the receipts. Sloane's phone pinged relentlessly as the evidence poured in.

Sloane stared at it, heart hammering. "This is enough to bury them."

"Good," Tessa said. "Now we do it the right way."

Graham's phone rang—Navarro.

He answered. "Navarro."

Navarro's voice was urgent. "The board is calling an emergency community meeting tonight. 'Safety and School Partnerships.'"

Tessa laughed without humor. "Translation: they're going to paint Sloane as a threat publicly."

Navarro lowered his voice. "Clayborn is pushing for it."

Graham's eyes went flat. "We'll be there."

Navarro hesitated. "Graham… it's going to be ugly."

Sloane swallowed, then said clearly, "Good."

Everyone looked at her.

Sloane's hands still shook—but her voice didn't.

"They've made me small my whole life," she said. "I'm done. If they want a show, I'll give them one."

Graham's gaze warmed—proud and worried at the same time. "Sloane…"

She looked at him. "Front and center."

He nodded. "Front and center."

The community meeting was held in the school gym—fluorescent lights, folding chairs, the smell of old basketball sweat and fresh politics.

The room was packed.

PTA moms. Coaches. Teachers. Local business owners. A few teenagers filming because nothing in Willow Creek was real unless it was on a story.

Sloane walked in with Graham at her side, Tessa on her other, Piper holding her hand like a tiny commander, and Miles walking close with a folder labeled EVIDENCE.

Heads turned.

Whispers started.

Sloane's heart pounded, but she kept walking.

Front.

Center.

Clayborn stood at the front with a microphone, calm as a man who thought the room belonged to him. Mindy sat in the front row, eyes red again, hands clasped like she'd been cast as "tragic wife."

The principal of the board introduced Clayborn like he was royalty.

Clayborn smiled. "We're here because we care about safety."

Sloane's mouth tightened.

Clayborn continued, voice smooth. "Rumors have circulated. Concerns about adult content, alcohol exposure, and business partnerships—"

Graham's hand squeezed hers, just once. Steady.

Clayborn gestured magnanimously. "We will consider distancing school events from businesses that don't align with our family values."

Murmurs.

Sloane's stomach turned.

Then Clayborn added, like a dagger: "And we are investigating reports made to CPS."

The room gasped.

Piper's hand tightened on Sloane's. "Mom," she whispered.

Sloane's breath caught—but then something in her snapped into clarity. Rage can be a compass, if you let it.

She raised her hand.

The moderator blinked. "Yes, ma'am?"

Sloane stood.

The room quieted in that charged way it does when people sense a woman about to either crumble or combust.

Sloane smiled politely. "Hi. I'm Sloane Matthews. Owner of MILF & Cookies."

A few laughs—nervous, supportive.

Clayborn's smile tightened.

Sloane continued, voice calm. "Before you 'distance' yourselves from me, I'd like to offer facts."

Clayborn lifted a hand. "This is not the place—"

"Oh, it is," Tessa muttered loudly enough for three rows to hear.

Laughter flickered.

Sloane held up her phone. "This week, my bakery was targeted with false complaints, sabotage, and an attempt to frame me with misuse of county vendor credentials. I have security footage. I have emails. And I have messages."

Clayborn's jaw clenched.

Sloane looked around the room. "And because the rumors escalated to a CPS report involving my child, I am not staying quiet anymore."

A hush fell.

Sloane turned slightly and nodded at Miles.

Miles stepped forward like a tiny attorney and handed a folder to the moderator.

"My dad says evidence matters," Miles said.

Graham blinked, startled, and Sloane's heart squeezed.

The moderator opened the folder, eyes scanning.

Clayborn's voice sharpened. "Those materials may be—"

Sloane cut in, still calm. "They are screenshots of text messages from Mr. Clayborn discussing how to make allegations 'look organic' and how to use 'child safety optics' to pressure the school."

The room's noise changed. Less whispering. More what the hell.

Mindy's face went paper-white.

Clayborn's smile faltered—just a hair.

Sloane continued. "I also have texts from my ex-husband admitting he used my name for county vendor access, which was then used in the sabotage framing."

Gasps.

Someone muttered, "That's insane."

Sloane nodded. "Yes. It is."

Clayborn stepped forward, voice tight. "This is a smear campaign —"

Sloane's eyes locked on his. "Funny. That's what you

called mine."

A ripple of laughter and shock moved through the crowd.

Clayborn's face reddened.

Sloane lifted her phone again. "I posted a video earlier today stating that if anything happens to my child after this, everyone will know where to look. That's not a threat. That's accountability."

Clayborn's voice turned sharp. "This is harassment."

Graham stood then—tall, controlled. "No. This is a woman defending herself against harassment."

Clayborn turned to him, eyes cold. "Graham, you're throwing away your reputation for—"

"For truth," Graham said. "For decency. For the fact that you don't get to use my son's school to destroy someone's life because you don't like her neon sign."

Applause started—small at first, then stronger.

A teacher stood. "We're tired of politics."

A dad stood. "My kids loved the bake-off. MILF & Cookies donated more than anyone."

A mom stood—one of the whisperers from earlier—voice shaking. "I shared that post. I didn't know. I'm sorry."
Mindy looked like she might faint.

Clayborn's composure finally cracked. "You're all being manipulated by—"

"By you?" Piper called out suddenly.

Every head turned.

Piper stood on her chair, tiny hands on her hips like she'd been practicing this speech in the mirror.

"My mom is not bad," she said loudly. "My mom is brave. And you're mean."

The gym went dead silent.

Piper continued, voice clear as a bell. "You should be ashamed."

Mindy's mouth fell open.

Clayborn looked like he'd swallowed a nail.

And then—because children are nuclear truth bombs—Piper added:

"And also my mom's cookies are the best, so… you're dumb."

The gym erupted in laughter.

Even the moderator choked.

Sloane covered her mouth, tears stinging her eyes—not from fear this time, but from the sudden, ridiculous relief of being seen.

Clayborn tried to regain control, but the room had shifted. You could feel it—like a tide turning.

Tessa leaned into the microphone the moderator offered, voice sweet and lethal. "We'll be providing all evidence to the county and pursuing legal action where appropriate. Thank you."

Clayborn stepped back, face stiff with humiliation.

Mindy—finally—stood, trembling. "I—" she started, voice cracking.

Sloane watched her, heart pounding.

Mindy swallowed. "I let this go too far."

Gasps.

Mindy's eyes filled. "I was angry. I felt threatened. I thought I was protecting… something. And I was wrong."

The room went very still.

Mindy turned to Sloane. "I'm sorry."

Sloane's chest rose and fell.

She didn't forgive her in a neat, pretty bow.

But she nodded once. "Good."

Because sorry wasn't the ending.

Accountability was.

After the meeting, the crowd poured out buzzing like a disturbed hive. Phones were out. People whispered about lawsuits and resignations and how Clayborn might finally be done.

Sloane stood in the hallway, shaking, adrenaline fading.

Graham stepped close. "You were incredible."

Sloane swallowed. "I thought I might throw up."

He smiled softly. "You didn't."

She looked at him, eyes wet. "You stayed."

He nodded. "Always."

Sloane exhaled shakily. "I don't know what happens next."

Graham's hand found hers. "Next, we protect your bakery. Next, we protect our kids. Next… we go home."

Sloane's throat tightened. "Home."

Graham's eyes held hers, steady as a vow. "With you."

She laughed through tears. "Okay."

And then—right as she let herself breathe—Navarro hurried down the hall, face pale.

"Graham," he said. "Sloane."

Graham's body tensed. "What."

Navarro swallowed. "CPS just called. They're coming… tomorrow morning. To your bakery."

Sloane's blood went cold.

"They want to interview you," Navarro said quietly, "on- site. Because of the allegations."

Sloane's hands started shaking again.

Graham's face hardened. "Let them."

Sloane whispered, terrified, "What if—"

Graham turned to her, voice low and unwavering. "We show them the truth."

Sloane stared at him, breath caught.

Then her phone buzzed—one last twist.

A message from New Girlfriend.

I'm sorry. I forgot one thing.
Clayborn isn't the top.
There's someone above him.
And they're not done.

Sloane's stomach dropped.

Graham read over her shoulder, jaw tightening.

Tessa swore. "Oh, hell."

Sloane whispered, "Who."

New Girlfriend replied instantly.

Brent Halvorsen doesn't work alone.
He reports to someone in Raleigh.
This is bigger than Willow Creek.

Sloane's lungs felt too small.

Graham's hand squeezed hers. "Okay." Sloane blinked. "Okay?"

Graham's eyes were flinty. "Okay. Then we go bigger too."

And for the first time, she realizes:

This wasn't just a town trying to shame her. This was someone trying to erase her.

CHAPTER
Twenty Seven
The
Inspection
of a
Life

The next morning, the bakery looked too cheerful for what was about to happen.

Sunlight hit the front window like it was trying to be kind. The neon sign—MILF in bright pink, & Cookies in frosting script—glowed like it had no idea the world had teeth. The pastry case was stocked, the counters spotless, the chairs neatly set.

Sloane had cleaned until her hands were raw.

Not because she had anything to hide.

Because when people come for your motherhood, your body forgets logic and goes straight to survival.

Graham arrived before the doors opened, carrying two coffees and a folder so thick it looked like it could file for its own zip code.

"Okay," Sloane said, taking the coffee but not drinking it. "Tell me we're not going to get judged by someone who thinks a bakery name is a crime."

Graham's face was calm, but his eyes were sharp. "CPS is supposed to be neutral. They respond to reports. They evaluate. They close them."

Sloane gave him a look. "Neutral like PTA moms."

Graham exhaled. "Neutral like professionals. And if they're not, we document that too."

Tessa arrived ten minutes later with a blazer, a legal pad, and the vibe of a woman who had already drafted a lawsuit in her head.

Piper was in the back with Miles, "helping" by putting rainbow sprinkles in a jar labeled JUSTICE.

Sloane tried to laugh.

It came out like a cough.

Then, right at 9:00 a.m., a gray sedan parked across the street.

Two people got out.

One woman. One man. Both carrying clipboards.

Sloane's stomach dropped.

Graham's hand found the small of her back, steady. "We breathe," he murmured. "Front and center."

The bell jingled as they entered. The woman—late thirties, practical shoes, calm face—offered a businesslike smile.

"Ms. Matthews?" she asked.

Sloane forced her voice steady. "Yes."

"I'm Ms. Porter," she said, showing an ID badge. "This is Mr. Darnell. We're with Child Protective Services. Thank you for meeting with us."

Sloane nodded like her throat wasn't closing. "Of course."

Porter looked around the bakery slowly, observing the space the way people do when they're trying to assess more than cleanliness. She saw the kids' corner with coloring sheets. The ingredient binders. The sign that read ADULT MENU ITEMS REQUIRE WRISTBAND from the bake-off, still taped behind the counter like a talisman.

Her gaze flicked to the neon.

Then to Sloane.

"Before we begin," Porter said gently, "I need to ask: do you feel safe right now?"

Sloane blinked.

The question disarmed her. Not because it was tender—but because it was direct.

Sloane swallowed. "Yes," she said. Then, honest: "I feel… watched."

Porter nodded once, as if that confirmed something she already suspected. "Okay. Thank you."

Mr. Darnell's tone stayed neutral. "The report alleges alcohol exposure, inappropriate content, and unsafe environment for a minor."

Sloane's chest tightened.
Graham spoke, calm. "We're prepared with documentation and evidence. We also have proof of sabotage and harassment that escalated into this report."

Porter's eyes sharpened slightly. "Sabotage."

Tessa stepped forward. "Yes. And we have security footage."

Porter glanced at Tessa. "You are?"

"Tessa Walsh," she said. "Attorney. And his sister." She nodded at Graham like he was a weapon she'd helped forge.

Porter's expression didn't change much, but her eyes brightened with something like relief.

"Okay," she said. "Let's proceed."

They sat at the front table. Sloane hated that the table she'd once imagined as warm and cozy now felt like an interrogation chair with pastries.

Porter asked about Piper's routine, school, health, supervision, and household. Darnell asked about business practices, how alcohol was stored, who had access, if minors were ever in contact with adult-only ingredients.

Sloane answered everything clearly, without defensiveness, even when her voice wanted to shake. She reminded herself: truth doesn't need theatrics.

Then came the question that sliced deeper than the rest.

"Ms. Matthews," Porter said softly, "has anyone ever accused you of being unstable before?"

Sloane's breath caught.

Graham's posture went rigid.

Tessa's pen paused.

Sloane forced herself to exhale. "Yes," she said. "My ex-husband. And the people who benefited from me feeling small."

Porter nodded like she'd expected that.

"Okay," she said. "And have you ever—"

"No," Sloane cut in gently. "I have never endangered my child. I have had hard days. I have had panic. I have had grief. But my daughter is safe."

Porter watched her carefully. Then glanced toward the back where Piper's laugh floated out—bright, unbothered, full of life.

"Can we speak with Piper?" Porter asked.

Sloane's heart stuttered. "Yes."

Piper came out wearing a tiny apron that read SPRINKLE SOLDIER. She waved like she was greeting fans.

Porter smiled. "Hi Piper. I'm Ms. Porter. Can I ask you some questions?"

Piper looked at Sloane like: Can I say the truth or the funny truth?

Sloane squeezed her hand once. "Just be you, baby."

Porter asked simple things: Does your mom cook? Do you feel safe? Do you ever see alcohol? Do people ever yell?

Piper answered with the brutal clarity of a child.

"My mom cries sometimes but she still makes dinner," Piper said.

Sloane's throat burned.

"Do you ever drink anything you shouldn't?" Porter asked.

Piper gasped like offended royalty. "No. I'm seven."

Darnell asked, "Have you ever seen your mom give alcohol to kids?"

Piper stared at him like he was confused. "That would be insane."

Graham coughed a laugh into his hand. Tessa didn't even try to hide her smile.

Porter asked one more question: "Has anyone been mean to your mom lately?"

Piper's face tightened. "Yes. Miss Mindy and her pickle friend."

Sloane blinked. "Piper—"
Piper shrugged. "She smells like pickles and lies. That's just… facts."

Porter's eyebrows lifted. "Pickle friend."

Piper nodded seriously. "She tried to go in the back hallway and I told her 'no' but she did anyway."

The room went still.

Porter looked sharply at Sloane. "When did that happen?"

Sloane's stomach flipped. "Last week," she said quietly. "And we have footage of her planting items."

Porter turned to Darnell. "We need to see that footage."

Sloane stood, hands shaking, and led them to the office. She pulled up the security camera recording and played it.

The moment the hooded woman looked at the camera, Porter leaned in, eyes narrowing.

"I know her," Porter said quietly.

Sloane froze. "You… what?"

Porter's face stayed calm, but her voice shifted into something more serious. "That's not a PTA mom. That's a contracted investigator who has been flagged before."

Tessa's head snapped up. "Flagged by who?"

Porter hesitated—then made a decision. "By the state. For overstepping authority. She doesn't work for our office."

Sloane's lungs went tight. "So she's… what? A private contractor?"

Porter nodded. "Someone hired her."

Graham's voice went cold. "By Clayborn."

Porter didn't answer directly—but her silence was loud.

Darnell leaned forward, voice measured. "Ms. Matthews, based on what we're seeing, the allegations regarding alcohol exposure are not supported."
Sloane's knees nearly gave out.

Porter nodded. "We'll document that. We'll also document the evidence of sabotage and harassment. And we will recommend the case be closed, pending standard procedure."

Sloane pressed her fingers to her lips, trying not to cry.

Then Porter added, softer: "You should file a separate report about targeted harassment. This is… coordinated."

Sloane's voice cracked. "Thank you."

Porter stood. "I'm sorry you went through this."

They walked out, leaving the bakery suddenly too quiet again.

Sloane stood in the office doorway, shaking. Graham came behind her and wrapped one arm around her—not hiding her, just holding her.

Tessa exhaled like she'd been holding her breath for a week. "Okay," she said. "We're vindicated."

Sloane whispered, "But someone hired a contractor."

Graham's jaw clenched. "Raleigh."

Sloane's phone buzzed.

An email.

From Brent Halvorsen.

Subject line: MISUNDERSTANDING

The message was one sentence:

If you want this to stop, meet me today. Alone.

Sloane's blood ran cold.

Graham's voice was immediate. "No."

Tessa's eyes flashed. "Absolutely not."

Sloane stared at the screen, heart hammering.

Because "alone" wasn't a request.

It was a threat dressed as an invitation.

PIPEr_SCHEDULE.pdf

Sloane opens it.

It's Piper's school schedule.

And beneath it, a single line:

WE KNOW WHERE TO FIND HER.

Chapter Twenty-Eight

The Woman Who Won't Leave

Sloane didn't remember sitting down, but suddenly she was on the bakery floor with her back against the cabinet, breath shallow and hands numb.

Graham crouched in front of her, face taut with restraint.

"Look at me," he said. "Sloane. Look at me."

She tried. She really tried. But her mind had gone somewhere old and dark where fear had teeth.

"They know her schedule," she whispered.

Graham's voice didn't break. "That doesn't mean they can touch her."

Tessa's tone was fast, controlled. "We call the police. We call the school. We lock this down."

Miles stood in the doorway like a little statue, face pale. Piper was behind him, chewing on a straw, blissfully unaware.

"What's happening?" Piper asked.

Sloane forced herself up, wiping her face, voice too bright. "Nothing, baby. Just adult boring stuff."

Piper narrowed her eyes. "That's what you say when it's not boring."

Graham stood and walked to Piper, kneeling to her level. "Hey," he said gently. "We're going to do a safety plan. It's not because you're in trouble. It's because adults sometimes act dumb."

Piper nodded solemnly. "Okay."

Miles raised a hand. "I would like to be included in the safety plan."

Tessa blinked. "You absolutely will."

Within twenty minutes, Tessa was on the phone with a detective. Graham was calling the school to arrange pickup protocols.

Sloane was staring at the email like it was a knife held inches from her daughter's throat.

Then the bell over the door jingled.
Sloane's blood went cold.

New Girlfriend walked in.

Alone.

No ex. No smugness. Her eyes were red, her face blotchy like she'd been crying in a car for an hour and didn't want anyone to know.

Graham's posture shifted immediately. Protective. Suspicious.

Tessa moved in front of Sloane instinctively. "You have got to be kidding me."

New Girlfriend held her hands up. "I'm not here to fight."

Sloane stared at her, exhausted. "Why are you here."

New Girlfriend swallowed hard. "Because I know who Brent reports to."

Silence.

Sloane's stomach dropped. "Who."

New Girlfriend's voice shook. "An individual named Avery Kline. Raleigh."

Tessa's brows lifted. "That's—"

Graham's eyes narrowed. "Kline Strategies."

New Girlfriend nodded. "Yes."

Sloane blinked. "What is that."

Tessa's tone went sharp. "Political consulting. Crisis management. Reputation control."

Sloane's blood ran cold in a different way. "So this is… a smear campaign."

Graham's jaw clenched. "It's a professional one."

New Girlfriend stepped closer, tears gathering. "Your ex… he didn't just 'talk' to people. He hired them. He paid them."

Sloane's vision tunneled. "Why."
New Girlfriend's voice cracked. "Because he's angry. And because Clayborn offered to 'help'—because he has elections, board positions, donors, whatever. They thought if they made you look reckless, they could push you out."

Sloane's hands shook. "Push me out… of town?"

New Girlfriend nodded. "Of the community. Of the school. Of everything."

Tessa whispered, "Oh my God."

Graham's voice turned deadly quiet. "How do you know this."
New Girlfriend wiped her face. "Because I found the invoice."

Sloane's breath hitched. "Invoice."

New Girlfriend nodded and pulled a folded paper from her bag like it weighed a thousand pounds. "He left it on his desk. He thinks I don't read things.

She held it out to Sloane.

Sloane unfolded it.

At the top: KLINE STRATEGIES
Below: Reputation Containment — Local Influence Operation
A line item: Target: S. Matthews (Willow Creek)
Another line item: Escalation Support: CPS trigger / Vendor credential misuse
Total: a number that made Sloane's stomach flip.

Sloane stared until the letters blurred.

Graham's voice was low. "That's criminal."

Tessa's eyes flashed. "That's a lawsuit. That's harassment. That's
—"

New Girlfriend's voice broke. "He said you deserved it.
He said you made him look bad by leaving."

Sloane's throat closed. "I made him look bad by
surviving."

New Girlfriend nodded miserably. "Yes."

Sloane swallowed hard, staring at the invoice. Rage rose
like heat under her skin. Not wild. Not chaotic. Clean and
focused.

Graham stepped closer to her, voice steady. "We don't
meet Brent alone."

Sloane nodded slowly. "No."

Tessa snapped, "We meet him with law enforcement."

New Girlfriend whispered, "He won't show if he knows."

Sloane lifted her eyes. "Then we make him think we're
alone."

Everyone went still.

Graham's gaze locked onto hers. "Sloane."

Sloane's voice was calm. "If he wants a meeting alone,
we give him one."

Tessa blinked. "That's insane."

Sloane looked at her. "No. It's strategy. He wants me
scared and isolated. He wants me to stop fighting. I'm
done giving people what they want."

Graham's jaw flexed. "I don't like it."

"I know," Sloane said softly. "But listen."

She held up the invoice. "This is bigger than my bakery now. This is bigger than Mindy. Bigger than Clayborn. Someone in Raleigh is running operations like my life is a file."

Graham's voice dropped. "And you want to bait them."

Sloane nodded once. "Yes."

Tessa's eyes narrowed, then—slowly—she smiled. "Okay."

Graham blinked. "Okay?"

Tessa's voice was lethal. "We let Brent believe Sloane is alone. But she won't be."

Sloane turned to New Girlfriend. "You're going to forward me every message you have. Everything. Time stamps. Payments. Names."
New Girlfriend nodded quickly. "I will."

Graham's gaze stayed on Sloane. "This is dangerous."

Sloane's voice softened, but didn't waver. "So was opening this bakery. So was leaving my marriage. I'm done living like fear gets to drive."

Graham stepped in close, forehead to hers for a beat, not caring who saw. "Then I'm driving with you."

Sloane's eyes burned. "Front and center."

Graham whispered, "Always."

Sloane turned to Tessa. "We meet Brent."

Tessa nodded. "We set a trap."

Sloane inhaled.

Then her phone buzzed again.

237

A text. Unknown number.

A photo.

Sloane opened it and went ice-cold.
It was Piper.

At school.

Taken from a distance.

Caption: TOO SLOW.

Sloane's breath vanished.

Graham's face turned feral.

Tessa snatched the phone. "Call the detective. Now."

Sloane's hands shook violently.
New Girlfriend started sobbing. "Oh my God."

Miles whispered, "Dad…"

And Sloane—Sloane stood up so fast her chair scraped,
eyes blazing through terror.

"They don't get her," she said, voice low and deadly.
"They don't get my child."

Graham's voice was rough. "We're going to the school."

Sloane nodded. "And then we burn this whole operation
down."

KLINE STRATEGIES — INVITATION ACCEPTED

Location attached.

Time: Tonight.

And below it, one line:

Come alone, or she pays.

The night everything exploded, I found Piper and Miles asleep on the bakery floor under a blanket fort made from aprons and flour sacks.

Piper's hand was curled in Miles's shirt like she was anchoring herself.

Miles had one arm thrown protectively across her like instinct.

I stood there longer than I meant to.

They weren't just friends.

They were each other's stability.

Two kids born from broken adults trying to build something softer than what we gave them.

And I remember thinking.
If this bakery burns down tomorrow, at least they found each other here.

Chapter Twenty-Nine

Tonight, We Bite Back

Sloane didn't cry. Not when the photo hit her phone, not when the message underneath it said come alone, or she pays. Her body did that cold, razor-sharp thing it only did when fear turned into purpose. The panic tried to rise, but something in her shut it down. Piper wasn't going to become another thing she survived.

Graham was already moving, keys in hand, phone to his ear, voice clipped. "Navarro," he said. "Lock the school down. Now. No pickup unless it's me or Sloane. Tell the front office to keep Piper inside the admin suite." He paced the tight space of Tessa's kitchen like it was a command center and not a home that still smelled like detergent and safety.

Tessa was on speaker with the detective, her tone so controlled it sounded like she'd already decided who was going to prison. "Yes," she said. "We have an invoice. We have a name. We have a timeline. And now we have a direct threat involving a child. That escalates it to immediate action." Her gaze met Sloane's for a beat, steady as steel, then flicked away as she listened.

Miles stood in the doorway, pale but steady, clutching his Evidence folder like a shield. Piper stood beside him chewing her straw, calm in the way children could be calm—like she assumed adults would do their jobs and keep her safe. She looked between them with a frown that was too old for seven.

"What's happening?" Piper asked again.

Sloane crouched and took her daughter's face in her hands. She forced her own expression into softness even as everything inside her went rigid. "Baby," she said, voice low and steady, "someone is being mean and we're going to stop them."

Piper frowned. "Like… grown-up mean?"

"Yes," Sloane said, smoothing her cheek. "But you're okay. I promise."

Piper studied her for a long second, then nodded with the solemnity of a tiny judge. "Okay," she said. "But if they're mean again, I'm allowed to say 'thumb,' right?" Sloane let out a breath that almost laughed and kissed her forehead. "Yes, ma'am."

Graham's hand settled on Sloane's shoulder, firm and grounding. Not permission, not control—just a quiet I'm here. "We're going," he said. "Now." They moved as a unit—Tessa, Graham, Sloane, Miles—out the door and into the car like this was war and they were done pretending it was just small-town drama.

The school looked normal from the outside. That was the sickest part. Kids running on the playground. Parents in pickup line. A teacher holding a coffee like the world wasn't on fire. Inside, Principal Navarro met them at the front, face tight.

"She's safe," he said immediately, like he knew Sloane's heart had fallen straight into her stomach and shattered there.

Relief hit Sloane so hard her knees nearly softened. Navarro led them into the admin suite, and there Piper sat at a small table coloring a cupcake with a sword, as if she'd decided the only reasonable response to danger was pastry warfare. She looked up, yelled "Mom!" with realization and launched herself into Sloane's arms like nothing had happened.

Sloane held her too tight and too long. Piper patted her cheek. "It's okay," she said. "I told Ms. Porter I'm not drinking alcohol. I'm seven." Graham made a sound that was half laugh, half pain, then turned away for a second like he needed to breathe somewhere private.

Navarro glanced toward the hall. "CPS is already aware this report looks malicious," he said quietly. "They're treating it as harassment." Tessa nodded like she'd expected that. "Good."

Sloane pulled back enough to look at Piper's face. "Did anyone talk to you today?" she asked. "Anyone you didn't know?"

Piper's brow furrowed. "There was a lady."

The room narrowed. Sloane's throat tightened around the

word. "A lady."

Piper nodded. "She was outside the fence. She said she liked my hair and asked if I wanted a cookie." Graham's entire body went rigid, and Sloane felt her blood go cold.

"What did you say?" Sloane asked, keeping her voice gentle.

Piper shrugged. "I said no because that's stranger danger and also I already ate a muffin." Miles whispered, "Good protocol," like he needed it said out loud. Sloane hugged Piper again, shaking now, because she couldn't not.

Navarro swallowed hard. "Security has the exterior cameras," he said. "We're pulling footage." Tessa's voice turned colder than the hallway tile. "That's your photo," she said. "That's how they got it."

A few minutes later an officer came in holding a printed still image. "Got her," he said.

Sloane leaned in. The image was grainy, the profile half- hidden by sunglasses, but the posture was unmistakable— the way the woman stood like she owned space. Sloane's stomach dropped because she had seen that posture before. Recently. Close. Not as a stranger at all, but as someone who'd smiled at her across a bakery counter and looked at her daughter like she was testing a weak point.

Graham stared too, eyes narrowing. Tessa's face drained. Sloane whispered, "That's—" and then the officer said the name out loud, reading from the visitor parking log.

"That's the woman who signed into visitor parking," he said. "Name listed as Avery Kline."

Silence detonated inside Sloane's skull. Avery Kline wasn't a rumor anymore. Avery Kline wasn't Raleigh. Avery Kline was in Willow Creek, close enough to offer Piper a cookie, close enough to remind Sloane that she could reach into her life whenever she wanted.

Sloane forced the words out. "Where is she now?"

"Gone," the officer said. "Left before we could stop her."

Graham's voice turned lethal. "We're not waiting."

Tessa's phone buzzed. She glanced down, then looked up, eyes wide. "The meeting," she said. "Kline Strategies invite. Tonight." Sloane's stomach flipped like gravity changed.

Graham looked at the officer. "We need a sting." The officer nodded once. "Already called in. If she threatened a child, we can move."

Tessa leaned toward Sloane. "You're not going alone."

Sloane's voice came out steady, even as her body wanted to shake apart. "No. But she thinks I will." Graham's face tightened. "We do it smart." Navarro hesitated. "You sure?" Sloane's gaze hardened. "They took my bakery. They tried to take my reputation. They tried to take my motherhood. Tonight they don't take anything else."

They staged it like a movie, but it felt too real to be cinematic. The office suite downtown was sleek and intentionally calming, the kind of place where people ruined lives with polite emails and expensive suits. Detectives waited in plainclothes. Two officers held the hallway. A marked car sat around the corner like a promise.

Graham wanted to be the one walking in, and Sloane could feel it in the way his body kept angling toward the door like he could physically block harm. But Sloane was adamant. "She asked for me," she said. "I'm the bait. I'm the proof." Graham's jaw worked. "I hate this." Sloane met his eyes. "But you trust me?" His stare cut through her. "Yes. I trust you. I don't trust them."

Tessa adjusted the mic at Sloane's collar. "Remember," she said quietly, "you don't argue. You don't confess. You get her talking." Sloane nodded once, then walked in.

Brent Halvorsen waited at the table, smiling like a man who could blend into any crowd and destroy you from inside your email inbox. "Ms. Matthews," he said. "Thank you for coming."

Sloane didn't sit. "You threatened my child."

Brent's smile didn't move. "No. I offered you an opportunity to end this."

"By coming alone."

"It's cleaner," he said, like he was discussing dry-cleaning.

Sloane kept her voice flat. "Who hired you."

Brent's eyes flickered. "You already know."

"Avery Kline."

"That's the name," he said, a little too pleased.

Sloane leaned forward a fraction. "You planted liquor. You filed false reports. You used my identity for a county badge. You leaked edited footage." Brent folded his hands. "Your ex provided your information. Your town provided the platform. All we did was amplify."

Sloane felt bile rise. "All you did."

Brent leaned in. "You were a risk."

"To what?"

Brent's smile thinned. "To control."

Sloane held his gaze. "What does my bakery have to do with control?"

"You've got influence," Brent said. "People like you—messy, likable, loud—become symbols. And symbols are inconvenient when certain people need a community to follow a specific narrative." He said it like it was a marketing strategy instead of a threat.

"Clayborn paid you," Sloane said.

Brent's gaze slid away. "Clayborn paid. Your ex pushed. But Clayborn isn't the top."

Sloane's heart pounded. "Then who is."

Brent's smile returned, calm and almost admiring.

"You're finally asking the right questions." The door clicked behind her.

Heels. Perfume. Poise.

Sloane turned, and her blood turned to ice because it wasn't Mindy and it wasn't Clayborn. It was New Girlfriend—

the woman who'd stood in Sloane's bakery and smiled like she wasn't holding a knife behind her back.

"Hi, Sloane," she said gently. "I'm sorry it had to get this messy."

Brent stood like a man greeting his boss. "Ms. Kline," he said.

Sloane couldn't breathe. "You're—"

"Avery," the woman said. "Avery Kline."

Sloane forced air into her lungs. "You were in my bakery. You were at the school."

"Yes," Avery said, expression unchanged.

"You lied."

"It wasn't personal."

"You threatened my child."

Avery's eyes cooled. "You were supposed to quit after the first wave. But you didn't. You got louder. You got more beloved." She leaned closer. "You became a problem."

"Why me," Sloane whispered.

Avery's smile sharpened. "Because you don't know what you are."

"I'm a tired mom with a bakery," Sloane snapped.

"No," Avery said softly. "You're a witness." The word hit something locked in Sloane's mind and rattled it.

"A witness to what," Sloane asked, voice shaking.

Avery didn't blink. "Years ago, you sat in a hospital waiting room and you saw something you weren't supposed to see." Sloane froze. The air went thin again, the way it did before a memory surfaced.

"What did I see," Sloane whispered.

Avery's gaze flicked down to Sloane's collar, and for the first time her expression changed. Recognition. The mic. She smiled wider, not afraid, almost amused. "That's cute," she murmured. "You brought witnesses."

Sloane stepped back. Her voice turned deadly. "You should know something about me. I don't comply." Avery's eyes narrowed. "You will."

Sloane shook her head. "No."

The door burst open. Detectives flooded the room, fast and controlled. "Avery Kline," an officer barked. "Hands where we can see them." Brent's face drained. "Wait—" Cuffs snapped around his wrists. Avery lifted her hands slowly, smile still intact, as if someone had spilled coffee on her laptop.

Graham appeared in the doorway behind the officers, eyes locked on Sloane like a lifeline. She stumbled to him, and he caught her immediately. "You're okay," he murmured. "You're okay."

Avery turned as officers guided her out. She looked directly at Sloane and smiled—not defeated, not afraid. Satisfied. "You still don't know what you witnessed," she said softly, for Sloane alone.

Sloane's blood went cold, because Avery didn't look like a woman who'd lost. She looked like a woman who'd advanced the board.

Chapter Thirty

The Final Ingredient

Willow Creek woke up hungry. Hungry for drama, for a villain, for a headline to share with coffee and moral superiority. But for the first time in weeks, the story didn't belong to the PTA. It belonged to the truth.

The county issued a statement about targeted harassment and vendor badge fraud. Police confirmed arrests tied to false reporting, identity misuse, and child endangerment. Mindy Clayborn deleted her pinned boycott post and replaced it with an apology that sounded like it had been written by someone holding her phone at legal gunpoint. By lunchtime, she resigned. The Moms Group—once a coliseum—turned into an apology parade full of people using words like "concerned" to cover the shape of what they'd done.

Sloane reopened the bakery anyway. Not because she was ready, but because she refused to let them train her out of her own life.

A line formed out the door. People brought flowers. Someone brought a poster that read WE STAN OUR LOCAL MILF. Sloane laughed so hard she cried, then cried for real in the back storage room where no one could see, because relief had its own grief inside it.

The CPS case was closed. The detective confirmed the report was malicious and connected to burner emails linked to Brent's firm. The liquor "evidence" was officially logged as planted. The inspector follow-up was flagged as manipulated scheduling through county vendor systems. The town moved on, because towns always did.

But Sloane didn't.

Avery's last words kept echoing: You still don't know what you witnessed. Sloane could feel the memory like a bruise she couldn't press. A shadow behind her eyes. Something she had trained herself not to look at, because the divorce had already taken everything she could handle.

That afternoon, while Piper and Miles decorated cupcakes in the corner and Sugarloaf licked frosting off the floor like this was just another Tuesday, Graham came in through the back door with rain in his hair and his sleeves rolled like he was bracing for impact. He set a small box on the counter.

Sloane blinked. "What is that."

Graham's smile was soft, nervous, real. "A key."

Her chest tightened. "To what."

"My house," he said quietly. "Not as pressure. Not as a demand. Just… an invitation. For when you're tired of fighting alone."

Sloane stared at the key like it was both terrifying and holy. "You sure?" she asked.

Graham nodded once. "I'm sure."

Sloane's eyes filled, and then Piper ran up and yelled, "DOES THIS MEAN HE'S OUR DAD NOW?"

Graham choked. Sloane burst out laughing. "Piper!" Piper shrugged. "I'm just clarifying." Miles appeared behind her, calm as a tiny therapist. "She's processing through direct questions." Graham wiped his face. "We can discuss timelines." Sloane laughed through tears. "Yes. Timelines."

Graham leaned in and kissed her temple, gentle and grounding, and for one small moment it felt like an ending.

Then the bell jingled.

Tessa walked in, and Sloane knew instantly something was wrong—not because Tessa looked panicked, but because she looked stripped of sarcasm. Not lawyer-busy. Not coffee-deprived. Something worse.

"Tessa," Graham said, straightening.

Tessa swallowed hard. "We have a problem."

Sloane's stomach dropped. "What kind."

Tessa held up a manila envelope. No return address. Just Sloane's name in neat handwriting. Sloane's blood went cold.

"How did she get that delivered if she's in custody," Graham asked, voice low.

Tessa shook her head. "That's the point. Open it."

Sloane tore it open with shaking hands. Inside was a flash drive, a printed photo, and a single sheet of paper. Sloane's eyes landed on the photo first and her breath vanished.

It was her, years ago, sitting in a hospital waiting room. Face swollen from crying. A blanket around her shoulders. Divorce era. Seated beside her was a woman in scrubs, hair pulled back, smiling gently.
A woman Sloane didn't remember.

Sloane swallowed. "Who is that."

Tessa's voice tightened. "Turn the paper."

Sloane did, and the words punched the air out of her lungs: You didn't get targeted because of a bakery. You got targeted because you were a witness. You just don't know it yet.

Sloane's hands began to shake violently. Graham's voice dropped. "A witness to what."

Sloane stared at the photo again. Hospital. Waiting room. A day her mind filed away under survival. The memory wouldn't come fully, but she felt the edge of it—the smell of antiseptic, the sting of humiliation, the sensation of being watched.

Tessa pointed at the background of the photo. A man in a suit, half-turned but visible enough.

Sloane blinked. Her stomach dropped. "I know him," she whispered.

"Who," Graham asked.

Sloane's throat tightened. "Daniel Mercer." The school board chair. The man who shook hands at fundraisers. The man who smiled at the bake-off like he'd invented community.

Tessa nodded once, grim. "Now open the drive."

Graham shook his head. "Not here."

Sloane's voice was barely audible. "Yes. Here."

Tessa pulled a laptop from her bag like she'd been born ready for plot twists and plugged the drive in. A folder opened automatically. A single video file played.

Hospital security footage. The same waiting room. Sloane on the bench, face in her hands. Mercer speaking to the nurse in scrubs, handing her an envelope. The nurse nodding, then walking directly toward Sloane.

Sloane watched herself accept the envelope and open it. Her face changed—shock, fear, recognition—then she stood abruptly and walked out of frame.

Sloane's hand flew to her mouth. "I don't remember this," she whispered.

Graham's voice went rough. "Sloane…"
Tessa paused on the nurse's face and zoomed in. Sloane's blood went cold.

Because the nurse in scrubs was Avery.

For a second, the room disappeared. Not dramatically. Not in a cinematic way. Just… quietly. Like someone dimmed the lights inside my skull. I remember that waiting room. Not in photographs. Not in timestamps.

In feeling.

I remember the weight of my body. The way my back ached from carrying Piper for six months. The way my fingers trembled every time someone said the word custody. I remember the vending machine humming. I remember thinking: I am too tired to fight anyone. And then I remember her. She didn't feel suspicious. She felt kind. She brought me water in a paper cup and said I looked like someone who survives storms. I thought she meant emotionally. I didn't know she meant strategically.

In the video, I watched her hand me an envelope. And suddenly I remembered that too. It wasn't divorce paperwork. It wasn't custody.
It was a printout.

A screenshot of a contract.

A transfer.

Something between a man in a suit and a hospital administrator.

I didn't understand it then. I just knew it felt wrong. And I remember looking up from that paper and seeing him. The man in the background. Watching me notice. That's why he looked startled.

That's why she moved quickly after that.

I didn't forget because it wasn't important. I forgot because I was overwhelmed.

Because my marriage was ending.
Because I was pregnant.
Because survival was louder than suspicion.

But now?

Now I understand.

I wasn't targeted because I opened a bakery.

I was targeted because I saw something I wasn't supposed to see.

And they realized it the second my face changed in that waiting room.

But, there she was YEARS ago. Already in her life. Already watching. Already placing something in her hands.

Sloane's voice shook. "She knew me before."
Graham's face went hard. "This wasn't random."
Tessa's eyes widened. "This wasn't a local smear campaign."

Sloane stared at Avery frozen on the screen, smiling like a friend. The truth slid into place like a blade: Avery hadn't infiltrated her life as "New Girlfriend." Avery had been orbiting her for years, waiting for Sloane to become visible enough to be worth silencing again.

Sloane swallowed. "What did I see."

The screen flickered and another file loaded, title stark and final: WHAT YOU WITNESSED.

Before it could play, Sloane's phone buzzed.

Unknown number.

One last message: Welcome to the real story, Sloane. You've been running from it for years.

Sloane stared at the words, then looked up at Graham, and for the first time she understood why Avery had smiled while being arrested.

Because Avery didn't come to end her.

Avery came to activate her.

The hallway finally emptied.

The noise faded.

It was just the two of them in the fluorescent hum of aftermath.

Graham didn't let go of her.

"I need to say something," he said.

She pulled back slightly. "Okay."

"I should've stood up for you sooner."

That line connects to earlier conflict.

Then:

"I thought if I controlled the variables, nothing would explode again. After my wife died, after losing control once—I swore I'd never let chaos in." He said so softly. "But you aren't chaos," he says. "You're alive. And I kept trying to manage you instead of standing beside you."

And just when I thought I couldn't love this man any more… he explains, "I don't want precision anymore. I want real. I want you. Forever."

Chapter Thirty-One

Witnessed

Sloane didn't sleep. She sat in the office long after closing, the laptop open, the file paused like a bomb waiting for permission. Graham sat beside her, close enough that their shoulders touched. He didn't push. He didn't rush. He simply stayed, the way he always stayed when she needed something solid.

Tessa paced twice, then stopped. "If this is what I think it is," she said quietly, "we need the detective here."

Sloane shook her head. "No. I'm done letting people decide when I can handle my own story." She looked at the screen, then at Piper through the office window, laughing as she frosted a cupcake in the shape of a crown. "I'm not handing my life back to anyone."

Graham's hand tightened around hers. "You don't have to do it alone."

"I'm not," Sloane said, and hit play.

The video was grainy at first, the kind of footage that looked boring until you knew what to look for. Mercer moved through the hospital hallway with the relaxed confidence of a man who had never been told no. Avery— still in scrubs—walked beside him like she belonged there. They paused at a doorway. Mercer handed her an envelope. Avery nodded.

Then Mercer glanced toward the waiting room.

Toward Sloane.

He smiled.

And it wasn't friendly.

It was a smile that said: she doesn't know yet.

Avery walked to Sloane and sat beside her. The camera couldn't hear what they said, but it didn't need to. Sloane watched her past self accept the envelope and open it, and the way her face changed made her stomach turn. Recognition. Fear. The sudden realization that her divorce wasn't just a divorce.

She stood too fast and moved out of frame.

The footage cut to a hallway camera. Sloane walked quickly, clutching the papers inside that envelope. Mercer followed—unhurried, certain. Avery appeared at the other end of the corridor, not chasing, not rushing, simply blocking.

Sloane watched herself back up. Watched Mercer speak. Watched him lean in too close.

Then she saw the moment she'd buried.

Mercer's hand lifted, offering something—an agreement, a promise, a bribe, a threat. Sloane shook her head. Mercer said something again, and Sloane's past self went still in a way that made present Sloane feel sick. The words were silent, but the effect wasn't. Sloane's hands dropped. Her posture slackened. She nodded once, like she'd just been told the one thing she couldn't survive being true.

Graham's breath changed beside her. "He threatened Piper," he said, voice low.

Sloane's throat tightened. "Piper didn't exist yet." She stared at the screen. "He threatened… custody. He threatened to ruin me. He threatened to make sure I never got out." Her eyes burned. "He threatened something I would fold for."

Tessa's voice went cold. "He threatened to erase you."

The video cut again to a parking lot camera. Sloane walked to her car with the envelope and got in. Mercer stood behind her vehicle watching her drive away. Avery stood beside him. They spoke briefly, then Mercer handed Avery another envelope. Avery nodded. Then they walked back inside like nothing had happened.

Sloane stared at the screen, shaking. "So what did I witness in the envelope?"

Tessa clicked to the next file. Scanned documents appeared—financial ledgers, bank transfers, LLC names. A cluster of transactions that ran through shell companies. One name kept reappearing: Daniel Mercer. Another: Kline Strategies. The "charter expansion" fund. The vendor procurement line. The county badge system.

Graham exhaled slowly. "Money laundering through school and county channels."

Sloane's stomach rolled. "And my ex was connected."

Tessa nodded. "And when you got that envelope, you had proof." She looked at Sloane. "But you were in divorce survival mode. You were exhausted. You were easy to intimidate."

Sloane swallowed. The shame tried to rise, but she crushed it. "So Avery embedded herself back then," she said quietly. "To make sure I didn't talk."
"And to make sure," Graham added, eyes hard, "that if you ever did become visible enough to matter, they could discredit you."

Sloane thought of the smear campaign, the planted liquor, the fake CPS report, the edited footage. It wasn't random cruelty. It was strategy. It was the same playbook—silence, shame, isolation, erasure.

She wiped her eyes with the heel of her hand. "That's why the bakery was a threat," she said. "Not because it was vulgar. Because it gave me community. It gave me a platform. It made people believe me."

Tessa nodded. "Exactly."

Sloane's phone buzzed again, but she didn't jump this time. She didn't run. She didn't shrink. She stared at the screen and felt something settle into place—something hard, something clear.

She looked at Graham. "We take this to the detective."

Graham nodded. "Tonight."

"And Mercer," Sloane said, voice steady, "doesn't get to keep smiling for fundraisers."

Tessa's mouth twitched. "Front and center."

Sloane stood and walked out of the office, back into the bakery where Piper looked up from her frosting crown. "Mom," Piper said, "are we okay now?"

Sloane crossed the room and pulled her daughter into her arms. "We're okay," she whispered into her hair. "And we're going to make sure nobody ever does this again."

Piper nodded like that made perfect sense. "Good," she said. "Because I still vote glitter war."

Sloane laughed—real this time. "Okay," she said. "Glitter war."

Then she took Graham's hand and walked toward the door, not running, not hiding, not shrinking. Walking like a woman who finally remembered who she was.

And what she'd seen.

Chapter Thirty-Two

Front and Center

Three months later. The bakery is packed.

Not scandal-packed.

Not boycott-packed.

Actual paying-customer packed.

There's a chalkboard out front that reads:

"UNDER NEW MANAGEMENT: SAME MILF."

Graham hates it but I, for one, refuse to remove it.

I am standing directly behind the counter, elbow-deep in frosting, when Piper yells:

"Mom! Miles says if you and Graham get married I have to share a last name!"

Miles replies calmly: "That's not legally accurate."

"No one is getting married today. We are simply surviving capitalism."

By the time the lunch rush hit, the bakery didn't look like a crime scene anymore. It looked like a comeback.

I finally replaced the old cracked display case — the one that had survived liquor planting, a boycott, and my emotional instability — with a sleek glass one that actually closed without wheezing like it needed therapy. It sparkled. It reflected the neon sign in soft pink halos. It made my cupcakes look like they belonged in a museum instead of a scandal.

Right above it, framed and slightly crooked because I hung it myself, was the newspaper article.

LOCAL BAKERY EXONERATED IN SABOTAGE INVESTIGATION

I may or may not have taken a red Sharpie and circled EXONERATED like it personally apologized to me. Twice.

Under the frame, in the center of the display, sat my newest creation:

Accountability Angel Food.

Light. Airy. Innocent-looking.

Spiked with bourbon.

Because healing doesn't mean boring.

By three o'clock, a group of college girls from the community college had formed a full-blown photo line under the neon sign. They were posing with cupcakes, duck-lipping next to the glowing "MILF," and tagging the bakery like it was a tourist attraction instead of the place the PTA tried to crucify me in.

One of them squealed, "Oh my God, this is the scandal bakery!"

I leaned over the counter and deadpanned, "Please say 'locally owned small business' instead. It sounds more tax-deductible."

They laughed. They bought six cupcakes. They asked for a group photo with me.

I stood there — flour on my jeans, frosting on my wrist, neon humming above my head — and realized something wild:

They didn't see a mess.

They saw a woman who survived one.

And for the first time since I pulled into this town in a U-Haul full of doubt and gas station donuts, the air inside the bakery didn't feel heavy.

It felt earned..

"Yeah, about that… I heard you were almost shut down."
I turned around to find one of my regulars with a look of worry.

I cannot help but smile at her and the worlds came out like vomit, "Almost doesn't count. I'm like a cockroach with better branding."

About that time Graham walks in. Sleeves rolled. Carrying paperwork.

He kisses me casually like he belongs there.

"Sir, this is a place of business."

"I'm aware." He sarcastically rolled his eyes.

"Good. Because I'm about to overcharge you emotionally."

"I cleared out the office at my place. If you want to move your stuff in slowly… no pressure."

Sloane stares, "Define slowly."

"As slow as you need."

Smirking at him. Blushing at him. I've found peace. SO MUCH PEACE.

Piper and Miles are in the heat of a bake-off rivalry.

Pipers cookies: "Justice Sprinkle Surprise."

Miles creates: "Strategic Chocolate Compliance Bars."

Graham and I just giggle while they argue over branding.

And, in that moment I realize they aren't scared anymore.

They're loud.

They're normal.

The last of the costumers come and they go as we work together to clean the place to opening standards for the morning.

The neon sign glows.

But this time, I'm not crying.

I'm just tired.

Happy-tired.

"There's no manual for starting over after a divorce." I remind Graham, "But there should be one for winning anyway."

"You'd ignore it."

"Correct." I agree, as a smirk appears on my face.

"Mom?"

"Yes?" I respond to Piper.

"If you and Graham break up, can we keep him?"

"Excuse me?" Laughing.

"Statistically, he's the stable one." Miles butted in.

"I'm right here." Graham exclaims as he throws his hands in the air.

"Fine. But I'm keeping the bakery in the divorce."

Graham grabs my hand, twirls me to the front of MY cookie showcase and says, "Front and center".

"Always", I wink.

But this time it's not defiant.

It's peaceful.

SO FUCKING PEACEFUL.

Acknowledgments

Writing this book felt a little like opening a bakery in a town that isn't sure it wants you there — terrifying, exhilarating, and absolutely worth it.

To the early readers who said, "Keep going," when I was convinced I'd written chaos instead of a novel — thank you for your honesty, your red pen marks, and your belief in Sloane before I fully believed in her myself.

To the women who rebuild quietly, loudly, imperfectly, and without permission — this story belongs to you. You are not too much. You are exactly enough.

To the people who supported this book in the messy middle — who let me talk through plot twists, hospital scenes, frosting metaphors, and revenge arcs like they were real events — thank you for treating this story like it mattered.

To Piper and Miles — fictional, but fiercely real in my heart — thank you for reminding me that courage sometimes looks like glitter and sometimes looks like logic.

And finally, to anyone who has ever started over with nothing but stubborn hope and a slightly unhinged business idea (as I have had many) — I hope you keep building.

Front and center.

Always.

— Ray Gray

Also by Ray Gray

MILF & Cookies

A Small-Town Scandal Romance

Coming Soon:

Hexes and Exes
A laugh-out-loud romantic mystery about second chances,
bad decisions, and the kind of magic that doesn't come
with instructions.

More chaotic women.
More morally gray men.
More small-town secrets.

About the Author

Ray Gray writes romantic comedies with sharp humor, emotional depth, and just enough chaos to keep things interesting. Her stories feature women who refuse to shrink, men who learn how to show up, and small towns that can't keep a secret.

She believes frosting is a coping mechanism, second chances are earned, and happy endings should feel intentional.

When she's not plotting scandal or redemption arcs, she's probably overanalyzing dialogue, testing dessert recipes, or building the next fictional woman brave enough to be front and center.

If you enjoyed MILF & Cookies, don't miss what's coming next.

Follow Ray Gray on Amazon to be notified of new releases, exclusive updates, and more small-town chaos.

FRONT AND CENTER, BITCH.